NEVER FOR HIM

HOPE VALLEY

A SMALL TOWN ROMANCE

JESSICA PRINCE

A Note from the Author

I'll admit that I'm tearing up a bit as I write this. When I first started the Hope Valley series, I knew it was going to be the kind of series that would take over my world, and it certainly didn't disappoint in that.

Since 2019, this town and these characters have been such a massive part of my life, that the thought of saying goodbye hurts.

I love the note we ended on. I couldn't imagine going out with anyone other that Hunter and Serenity, and I feel like this was a high note for Hope Valley. I hope I did your man Hunter justice, and that you loved their HEA as much as I did.

That said, I'm struggling with the thought of letting this world go. I just can't do it.

Early in my career, I said I'd never do a legacy series. Well, turns out, I spoke too soon, because that is exactly what I'm going to do.

Coming soon (hopefully 2024) we'll be returning to Hope Valley with the stories of some of your favorite HV kiddos. This includes familiar faces from Hope House.

I hope that you're as excited about this new journey as I am, and in the mean time, happy reading!

~Jess

DISCOVER OTHER BOOKS BY JESSICA

WHITECAP SERIES
Crossing the Line
My Perfect Enemy

WHISKEY DOLLS SERIES
Bombshell
Knockout
Stunner
Seductress
Temptress

HOPE VALLEY SERIES:
Out of My League
Come Back Home Again
The Best of Me
Wrong Side of the Tracks

Stay With Me
Out of the Darkness
The Second Time Around
Waiting for Forever
Love to Hate You
Playing for Keeps
When You Least Expect It
Never for Him

REDEMPTION SERIES

Bad Alibi
Crazy Beautiful
Bittersweet
Guilty Pleasure
Wallflower
Blurred Line
Slow Burn
Favorite Mistake

THE PICKING UP THE PIECES SERIES:

Picking up the Pieces
Rising from the Ashes
Pushing the Boundaries
Worth the Wait

THE COLORS NOVELS:

Scattered Colors
Shrinking Violet

Love Hate Relationship
Wildflower

THE LOCKLAINE BOYS (a LOVE HATE RELATIONSHIP spinoff):
Fire & Ice
Opposites Attract
Almost Perfect

THE PEMBROOKE SERIES (a WILDFLOWER spinoff):
Sweet Sunshine
Coming Full Circle
A Broken Soul

CIVIL CORRUPTION SERIES
Corrupt
Defile
Consume
Ravage

GIRL TALK SERIES:
Seducing Lola
Tempting Sophia
Enticing Daphne
Charming Fiona

STANDALONE TITLES:

One Knight Stand
Chance Encounters
Nightmares from Within

<u>DEADLY LOVE SERIES:</u>
Destructive
Addictive

ONE

SERENITY

When I moved to Hope Valley, it had been in the hopes that whatever had been in the water that rained so much goodness down on my baby sister, Stella, would somehow find its way to me. After the past several months, I figured I was more than due for a bit of goodness.

Sure, from the outside looking in, my moral compass might have come off as a little shaky. And, yes, up until a couple months ago, I'd done some questionable things, but I wasn't a bad person. Everything I'd done had been to protect the people I loved. I hadn't liked the role I'd been tasked to play. In fact, I despised it to the point the sensation of my skin crawling had become a constant thing I'd had to learn to deal with.

But there wasn't anything I wouldn't do for my family. Seeing any one of them hurting caused a physical pain inside of me. That was the *only* reason I'd allowed them to talk me into doing the things I'd done.

You see, the Ryans came from a long line of grifters and con artists that dated back to the Pilgrims coming over on the Mayflower, or so rumor told. Truthfully, I hadn't had the patience to research just how far back it really went. But anyway, the craft had been passed down from generation to generation. My siblings and I had grown up in the life, learning different cons from the time we were in diapers.

Each of us had a specific role to play. Stella was the smart one. She had a gift for reading people and situations and had hands that were so fast and feather light, not a single mark ever felt their wallets or watches being nicked. My older brother, Spencer, was the clever one. He could talk people around to his way of thinking with minimal effort. You could have been standing in front of a bright red barn, but by the time he was finished, you would have been convinced it was purple simply because he'd said so. He could fleece you blind without you even realizing he'd done it.

And me, well, I was the pretty one.

That was all my worth seemed to be marked by. I wasn't smart like my little sister or cunning like my big brother. I was pretty, that was it. That was my claim to fame. I could dazzle men long enough for my family to bleed them dry. I was a deft hand at twisting them into compromising positions that would come in handy if we ever needed excellent blackmail material. It seemed the only tools I had at my disposal were my body and face, at least to everyone around me. The fact I looked good in a skirt was all that was required of me.

And I hated it.

Despite being able to pull off each job without actually letting a mark touch me, I'd still go home at night and stand beneath a scalding shower until every inch of skin on my body glowed bright red, and still, I couldn't seem to get clean. I might have played at seduction, but I wasn't a whore. I'd had sex with exactly two men in my life, so when it came to the con, I drew the line at anything physical. However, that didn't make me feel any better about what I was doing. It was as if there was a layer of grime over my skin that I would never be able to wash away.

People thought my looks were all I had to offer, and I'd spent my entire life smiling through the pain and hiding just how much that hurt.

Then everything changed a handful of months ago. It started with my father pulling a con on the wrong people and putting our entire family in danger. Fortunately, the story had a happy ending that came with my baby sister finding true love and all of the Ryans getting to step back from the life.

I was thrilled Stella found the man of her dreams and my brother got to focus on his wife and daughter without having to constantly look over his shoulder in fear that a con might have caught up with him. I loved that my folks had been able to sit back, relax, and enjoy their days with their kids and grandchild. But while everyone else had moved on, I'd been cast adrift.

I couldn't exactly use my grift skills in the real world, not that I'd wanted to. Walking away from that life had been the biggest blessing I'd ever experienced. I was grateful for a chance to do something else.

Anything else.

This was the fresh start I'd been wanting for as long as I could remember. Not having the first clue what I wanted to do with my life was terrifying, but I was determined not to waste this chance. I was going to grab hold and find the same damn happy my sister had, and I prayed this town was the first step in that.

I could have moved anywhere, but there was just something about the small mountain town that called to me. It was the beauty of the vibrant green mountains that surrounded the valley, the fresh smell of pine that filled my lungs with each inhale. Hope Valley felt magical, and every time I stepped foot in the town, I felt this sense of belonging that sank down into my bones. It was as if I were home.

Drawing in a deep breath, that crisp pine air invigorating me, I grabbed hold of the handle and pulled the door open, ready to take the second step toward my fresh start.

I'd been inside the Tap Room once before, but that had been at night when the place was buzzing with people and music as the drinks flowed. The jukebox was playing, only at a much lower volume, more like ambient noise carrying in the air below the murmured chatter. There was a decent size crowd, thanks to the fact that the place served lunch and dinner before things really picked up, but the vibe was much more sedate in the middle of a workday than it was on a Friday or Saturday night when people were looking to cut loose.

"Welcome to the Tap Room," the woman behind the bar greeted. She looked to be a few years older than I was, maybe early forties, but she wore her age well and would have been able to pass for years younger. Her personal style seemed to be a mesh of rocker, hippie, and country girl. It wasn't a combination I would have thought would work, but on her it totally did.

Her long, shiny black hair was pulled back into a stylishly messy French braid that hung over her shoulder, the ends of the multicolored scarf she was wearing as a headband twined through the strands. Another one was strung through the belt loops of her jeans. The stacks of bracelets on her arms jangled as she moved, and chunky silver and turquoise rings caught the overhead light as she rested her palms on the bar top in front of her. Her smile was warm and friendly as I moved closer. "What can I get you?"

"I'd really love a job if you have one of those available," I answered quickly. Putting it out there had to have been better than hemming and hawing. No need to waste anyone's time.

The woman's eyes narrowed, her gaze growing a tad more scrutinizing. She snapped her fingers like a lightbulb had just flipped on, declaring, "I knew you looked familiar. You're Stella Ryan's sister, right?"

My throat closed up at the mention of my sister's name, making it difficult to swallow. If this woman new Stella, odds were she already knew about our family's reputation. "Uh, yeah." I pushed my discomfort down so she couldn't see it. It was something I'd gotten damn good at. After all, a guy wouldn't buy that I was into him if I cringed every time he got close. I'd had to become an expert at hiding what I was feeling. I extended my hand across the bar. "Serenity Ryan, but most people call me Sere. Less of a mouthful."

There was no disgust or hatred in her gaze as she took my hand, giving it a firm shake. "Nice to meet you, Sere." Her words rang with sincerity. "I'm Rory Paulson. My husband, Cord, works at Alpha Omega."

Alpha Omega was a private investigation and security firm that had set up shop in Hope Valley some years back. Its reputation was well known far and wide, not only because the guys who worked there were the very definition of badass, known for getting the job done by any means necessary, but also because they were enjoyable as hell to look at.

Stella's new man, West, was part of the Alpha Omega crew, as was Stella herself. Once the owner of the place, Lincoln Sheppard, saw how my baby sister's grift skills could come in handy for some of their cases, he took her on too.

Stella had talked my ear off about her love for her new

job, as well as how awesome everyone she worked with was.

"Yeah, of course." I vaguely remembered her husband from the sorry excuse of a kidnapping my sister and I had been tangled up in several weeks back. It was a long story, but the gist of it was the man my father had conned just so happened to be connected to some pretty bad people. However, in an unexpected twist, he was also a world-class idiot who didn't have the first clue what he was doing.

West and his guys had busted in to save the day, but that was *after* Stella and I had already managed to get free and beat the living snot out of the pain in the ass. "It's nice to meet you too."

Casual as could be, Rory bent her elbows and rested her forearms on the wooden counter between us. "So, Sere. You got any experience waitressing or bartending?"

I let out the breath I hadn't realized I'd been holding until right that moment, when my lungs began to burn and the pressure in my chest built. The exhale slowly skated past my lips on a quiet whistle as relief swamped me that Rory wasn't the type of woman to judge or hold my past against me.

"I waited tables when I was younger. It's been a while, but I think I can pick it back up pretty fast. As for bartending, I can pull a beer like no one's business, but aside from that, my skills are pretty limited." My lips pulled into a line. "I'm not much of a mixologist. But I'm more than happy to make up for that by bussing tables," I added quickly. Anything to make myself the most appealing hire there ever was.

I wasn't sure why, but just like the town had called to me, the Tap Room was calling as well. Now that I'd gotten this far, any outcome that didn't end with me being newly employed at the local watering hole would suck.

"Well, lucky for you, this place is known for its beer." She waved her hand along the back wall where beer taps were lined from end to end, more brands and flavors than I'd known could possibly exist. "If it's cool with you, I'll start you on the floor for now. But on the off chance I need you behind the bar, one of the other bartenders or I will handle the more complicated orders. You can stick with pulling beers until you think you're ready to get your feet wet."

My eyes rounded and my jaw dropped. "Wait . . . I have the job?"

She let out a musical laugh, the sound nearly as beautiful as she was. "That's what you wanted, right?"

I pulled the corner of my bottom lip between my teeth and bit down. "Well, yeah. But—"

"You don't know this about me yet, but you will. I tend to follow my gut when it comes to meeting new people. It hasn't led me wrong so far, and my gut is telling me you're good people. I like your sister and she speaks highly of you." *Man,* but I had the best little sister in the world. "If you two are anything alike, I think this will work out perfectly."

I hoped she was right, because my gut was telling me this was exactly where I was supposed to be.

Two

T hree weeks later

I was standing at the back of the room, partially tucked away in shadows, hoping for a few seconds of peace. This was a joyous occasion, no doubt about it, and I was beyond thrilled that West had asked my baby sister to marry him, but I would have been lying if I said news of Stella's engagement hadn't brought a pang of envy that tended to flare up every now and then.

I didn't want to be jealous of my sister and the happiness she'd managed to find. It made me feel like I was the lowest of the low. If there was anyone on the planet who deserved a happily ever after, it was Stella. I just couldn't help but feel like I was being left behind.

Again.

She was getting married. Spencer's wife was newly pregnant with their second baby. And then there was me: a woman in her mid-thirties who tended bar and waited tables and didn't have a clue what else she wanted to do with her life.

"What are you drinking?" Stella asked as she skidded to a stop beside me, pulling me from the pity party I'd been hosting for myself. "Never mind," she blurted before I had a chance to answer. "Doesn't matter as long as it's alcohol." She snatched the glass from my hand and brought it to her lips before tossing her head back and downing nearly an entire glass of Cabernet in two large gulps.

I arched a brow as she let out an *aah* before wiping her mouth with the back of her hand. "You seem tense."

Stella hit me with a flat look. "That obvious?"

I smiled reassuringly and threw my arm around her shoulders. "Relax, babe. This is supposed to be a fun night."

She let out a huff of breath and sank into my side. "Easy for you to say. You're able to chill out back here. I'm stuck in the middle of it all."

My poor sister had never done well with being the center of attention, but given that the Tap Room was closed to the public tonight in order to celebrate *her* engagement, it was kind of hard for her to keep to the sidelines where she was most comfortable.

I felt for her, my heart going out and aching to protect

her like always. She was the youngest, the baby of the family, and I took my role as big sister and protector very seriously.

"I know it might not feel like it, but stepping out of your comfort zone like this is a good thing."

She cut her eyes to the side, her expression screaming *you're full of shit, and I can smell it.*

"It's true!" I insisted on a laugh. I waved my now wine-glass-less hand to encompass the entirety of the bar. "This is your engagement party, Stell Bell. All these people are here because they want to celebrate the fact that you found the love of your life." I didn't point out that the actual wedding day would be ten times worse. That little tidbit would surely have sent her spiraling. "They're here because they care about you and West."

At the mention of her fiancé's name, the tension and anxiety carved into my sister's face smoothed out and her expression went dreamy. That all too familiar pang shot through my chest at the sight of it, and I let out a silent sigh.

When the hell was it going to be my turn?

There had been a time in my life, years ago, when I thought that I'd found *The One*. Thoughts of the future filled my head, plans for our white picket fence and the two point five kids. I was so certain that was in the cards for me. Then the man who I thought loved me above all else went and smashed my heart to smithereens.

"I'm really lucky, aren't I?" Stella asked, her voice jerking me back into the present.

I clenched my arm, pulling her tighter against me in a sideways hug. "He's the lucky one, little sis. He landed you. No better prize out there."

She tilted her head, resting it on my shoulder. "Have I told you lately that I love you, Sere?"

All the envy bled out of me as I rested my head against hers. It was impossible for the love I had for my sister not to shine through anything else I might have been feeling. She was the kindest, most loving person you'd ever meet. A heart as pure as freshly fallen snow.

"Feeling's mutual, Stell Bell."

Just then I felt it, the prickling sensation skating across my skin that could only mean one thing.

I knew what I'd find even before I cast my gaze toward the entrance, and the mere sight of him never failed to make my heart race and my palms grow clammy.

The man actually made me nervous, something I hadn't thought possible given just how jaded I was. The things I'd done and seen when it came to the opposite sex had a way of stripping off the rose-colored glasses. But I could say with unwavering certainty that I'd never met a man like Hunter McCann in my life.

The first time I laid eyes on him, he'd left me breathless. Though, the same couldn't have been said had the shoe been on the other foot. I hadn't exactly been at my best at the time, what with having been kidnapped by a complete moron and all, but when Hunter busted into the warehouse where my sister and I were being held by what had to be the stupidest criminal on the face of the earth, an instant crush had formed.

Sure, he hadn't been the only one who came riding in to rescue us, in fact, he had the whole band of Alpha Omega badasses with him, and believe me when I say there was more eye candy to behold with that crew than one woman could handle. However, I'd only had eyes for him.

It wasn't just his looks, although, there was plenty of fine to go around. Everything from his sharp, masculine features to his rock-hard, muscle-bound physique looked like they'd been carved out of granite. If I'd had to guess, he cleared six feet by a good few inches, making me, a woman who stood at five foot seven and had a penchant for sassy stilettos, feel positively tiny in his presence. Just from looking at him, I knew he'd have been more than capable of tossing me over his broad shoulders and carrying me off to his lair, and *man* did I wish he would.

But in spite of how gorgeous he was, his eyes were what really drew me to him. The most beautiful eyes I'd ever seen. A blue so crisp they reminded me of melting glaciers. Those liquid pools carried such intense shadows, a shiver ran along my spine the first time his gaze connected with mine. I hadn't known it was possible for eyes as icy blue as his to hold storm clouds, but he proved me wrong.

He carried some kind of pain with him like a broody cloak he never took off. As demented as it might have sounded, something about those shadows called to me like my own personal siren song. I knew all about pains of the heart, and I wanted nothing more than to see if I could squeeze a little light out between the darkness lurking in his gaze.

There was just one teensy problem.

I wasn't anything more to him that the sister of his buddy's new fiancée.

Talk about a hit to a woman's pride. Still, I couldn't seem to turn the attraction off.

"Hey. Earth to Serenity." Stella snapped in front of my face, giving me a jolt.

I shook my head to clear it of the cobwebs Hunter always seemed to cause. "Sorry. Did you say something?"

Her forehead pinched in a frown as she studied me. "You totally spaced there for a second. What were you staring at?"

"Nothing," I answered quickly, but she was already leaning in front of me, following my earlier line of sight until her gaze landed directly on the very figment of every fantasy I'd had for weeks.

"Oh, Serenity," she said in a way that had my spine going ramrod straight. Her tone held a warning while her features dipped with pity.

"What?" I asked with a defensive snap to my tone. "Why are you looking at me like that?"

She twisted and stepped in front of me, placing her back to the room. "Look, sis, I want you to be happy. There's nothing I want more in this world than you to find a man to treat you how West treats me. But Hunter?"

My lips pulled into a frown of confusion. "What's wrong with Hunter? I thought you liked him."

"I do," she insisted vehemently. "I do like him. He's great, it's just . . ."

I crouched a bit to meet her downcast eyes. "Just what?"

"I don't know, he's just . . . hard, I guess. That's the only way I can think to explain it."

I shot her a sassy wink, attempting to lighten the tension that had suddenly swelled around us. "Figured you already knew this by now, but the harder the better."

She rolled her eyes and gave my arm a smack. "That's not what I mean, and you know it." She inhaled deeply, like she was trying to get her thoughts in order. "He's perfectly pleasant whenever we're at work together, but other than that, the man's a vault. He doesn't give anything away, and it's damn near impossible to get to know him."

So, he was the strong, silent type; if anything, that made him even more appealing to me. There was something about those hard, sexy, broody characters in the movies that drove women crazy. Hunter was a real-life version of every male heartthrob to ever grace the big screen, and I was just like all the hopelessly infatuated women in those movies, drawn to him in a way that couldn't—or maybe wouldn't—be ignored.

"There's nothing wrong with keeping your personal life private," I defended.

"No, there's not. But it's not just that." She shook her head in exasperation, like she was trying to click her thoughts into place like pieces of a puzzle. "I'm not sure there are many people—if any—who know everything there is to know about that man, and I'd hate to see you get hurt because he couldn't give you what you deserved."

My mouth curved upward as I grabbed hold of my sister and pulled her into a tight, bone-creaking hug. Her concern was the perfect example of that generous and loving heart of hers.

"I love you for caring, Stell Bell." Untangling her from my hold, I took her by the shoulders and pushed her back so we could see eye-to-eye. "But you don't need to worry about me." I winked to stress the point. "I'm a big girl. I know what I'm doing, trust me."

She didn't look convinced. "Really?" she asked archly, one brow rising.

I hemmed and hawed for a second. "Well, maybe not. But something tells me it'll be damn fun, at the very least."

She looked like she was about to argue when I was saved by the bell. Well, more aptly, I was saved by a six-foot-something hunk of man.

"I'm not interrupting, am I?"

I shifted my smile from my sister to her beloved fiancé. "Not at all." I gave Stella big, playful eyes. "We just finished up here. Right, little sis?"

"Great." West looked adoringly down at Stella, like she was the very reason the sun came up every morning and the moon shone bright at night. "I wanted to take my woman for a spin on the dance floor. How's that sound?"

If it had been anyone else asking, I was sure my little sister would have thought that to be a nightmare, but I got the distinct impression, when the two of them looked at each other, no one else existed.

Stella took West's hand, and together, the two of them started toward the dance floor as the song on the juke box switched to a slow ballad.

I watched them for a few seconds before leaving my cozy little nook in the back of the room and headed to the bar for a refill. I needed a little liquid courage for what I was about to do.

THREE
SERENITY

Anticipation buzzed beneath my skin, like my veins were a can of soda and the contents had been shaken up, ready to explode. It was a warm, fizzy kind of excitement I hadn't experienced in longer than I could remember, a thrill I thought was long since dead and buried.

I felt like a giddy schoolgirl in the cafeteria, psyching herself up to approach the captain of the football team, as I started across the bar in Hunter's direction. After all the men I'd conned: the ones with tan lines on their ring fingers, the ones who didn't bother taking their rings off at all, or my personal favorite, the ones who lied about their wives being dead when the recon my family had done proved the missus was alive and well, I didn't think it was possible to ever feel excitement about another man again. But Hunter made me feel it in a very big way.

Since I started working at the Tap Room, I'd seen him

come in a couple times a week. We'd exchanged pleasantries, but it was all surface. For weeks I'd been searching for an in, but so far I'd gotten nowhere. Some of those nights he'd have a drink or two before heading home. But it was the other nights that left stinging lashes against my skin. The man was single and free to do whatever—or in his case, whomever—he pleased. It wasn't a regular occurrence—but it wasn't exactly rare either—that, if a woman caught his eye, they'd end the night leaving the bar together after he picked up her tab. Those nights sucked. The only certainty I'd discovered after studying his patterns was that the women he left with usually disappeared after only a couple of encounters.

He sat on one of the round stools in front of the long bar, a few of the guys I recognized from Alpha Omega, Bryce and Marco, standing around him. As I grew closer, Bryce said something to Hunter, then chuckled and clapped him on the back before he and Marco took off, leaving him sitting alone. At least until I summoned up the nerve it took to go the rest of the way.

I rested my hand on the back of the empty stool beside his. "This seat taken?"

Those ice blue eyes came to me, the shadows still present.

"Hey, Wildcat," he greeted, using the term he and the rest of the guys at Alpha Omega had christened me with after my and Stella's kidnapping. They'd stormed into the warehouse to save Stella and me, only to find us beating the ever-loving shit out of the man who'd organized the entire abduction. While we were taking care of him, the guys were outside, taking care of the jerk's hired guns.

We'd been like two feral animals, tearing at the son of a bitch. Wild cats. It was a name well deserved and one I'd gladly wear like a badge of honor, because that meant I was a fighter. I was a wildcat. I could live with that, for sure.

He jerked his head toward the stool. "Take a seat. Make yourself comfortable."

I did just that, trying my best not to look too eager as I hopped into place. I watched from the corner of my eye as he brought the pint glass to his lips and drank the last of the beer inside.

Just then, one of the Tap Room's bartenders, a pretty, young brunette by the name of Mona, spoke up, drawing my focus away from the man beside me. She was sweet and bubbly, and I always had fun with her on the nights we shared the same shift. "Hey, lady. What can I get you?"

I started to push myself up, suddenly feeling strange at the thought of being waited on by one of my own co-workers. "Oh, I can get—"

She rolled her eyes and cut me off. "Please, it's your sister's engagement party. Don't you dare step foot behind this bar. It's your night off."

I smiled over at her, her kindness a gift she didn't even realize she was giving. I'd been seriously lacking when it came to girlfriends in my old life. It was nice to finally have people to talk to who weren't related to me by blood.

"Glass of red wine, please. Whatever bottle of Cab you

have open back there is fine." The Tap Room might have been famous for their beer, but that didn't mean they skimped on anything else. It turned out that Rory didn't just run the Tap Room, she owned it. It had been in her family for quite some time, and she'd inherited it from her folks when they retired a few years back. Only, they still came in on a regular basis to help out since Rory and her husband, Cord, had also started a group home for foster and at-risk kids called Hope House.

Those two had their plates incredibly full, but it was with so many incredible, kind-hearted things. To say I admired the hell out of the Paulsons would have been putting it mildly. They were good people. In fact, nearly everyone I'd met in Hope Valley over the past few weeks were good people. To the point it was giving me a bit of a complex. I wanted to belong, to be as good as all these people. I wanted to wash myself clean of the past and I was determined to do everything in my power to make that happen.

Mona looked at Hunter then, the apples of her cheeks growing pink as she asked, "Would you like a refill?" I had to bite the inside of my cheek to stifle a laugh. I felt for the girl, honestly. I understood that blush all too well. His potent brand of handsome was intoxicating for women of any age, even those a good fifteen years younger than he was.

He responded in the affirmative by grunting and pushing his empty glass in her direction.

I waited until Mona had brought my wine and

Hunter's fresh beer before I spoke again. "Not a big fan of engagement parties?"

He let out another grunt as he lifted the pint to his lips. "That's putting it mildly," he muttered around the rim of the glass before taking a pull, some unidentifiable meaning hidden beneath those words.

He wasn't really giving me much to work with, but I was determined, so I pushed onward. "I'm sure West and Stella wouldn't mind if you bailed early." I looked toward the dance floor where the two of them were still practically glued together, looking dreamily into each other's eyes as they swayed to the music. It would have been nauseating if I wasn't so damn happy for them. "I'm not sure they'd even notice if the whole bar cleared out."

He let out a sound that was a mix of a chuckle and a huff and gave a half-hearted shrug. "It's fine. Gotta drink somewhere, right?"

"True enough." Speaking of drinks, I lifted my wineglass and sucked back half the contents in an effort to embolden myself before I hopped off the stool, and ordered, "Come on."

He looked at me, his dark, heavy brow furrowed. "What?"

"If engagement parties aren't your jam, let's go play pool. Then you're just a guy hanging at the bar and it's no longer about the reason you're here."

One corner of his mouth trembled, like he was suppressing a grin, and I was hit with a sense of determination; I was going to pull a grin from him, a *real* grin, if it was the last thing I did. "It's that easy, huh?"

I smiled brightly, leaning over to bump his shoulder with mine. "Yep. It's that easy. And hey, maybe I'll even take pity on you and let you win a game or two. You know, for your pride."

Hunter McCann might have been the strong silent type, but I knew every breed of man there was, and they all had one thing in common.

They could never back down from a challenge.

Just as I'd hoped, Hunter took the bait just like the rest of them. "You'll *let* me win?"

I hummed and tapping my chin. "If I'm feeling charitable."

He turned his head, looking toward the back of the bar at the rows of pool tables. The alcove was surprisingly empty, except for Fletcher, the eighteen-year-old kid Rory had recently hired, who was clearing out empty bottles and glasses before wiping the tables down.

Looking back at me, Hunter rose from his stool, those eyes like a frozen-over winter lake shimmering with determination. "All right. Bring it, Wildcat. But I don't want to hear you whine when I kick your ass."

I threw my head back on a belly laugh. "Oh, honey. I'm not the one who'll be whining by the end of the night."

I eased the pool cue back, testing the weight and feel of it, the smooth wood gliding between my fingers as I braced for the break. Hunter stood at the other end of the table, the butt of his pool cue braced on the ground, his long, thick fingers knotted around the other end as he watched me closely. A grin teased at my lips; this was going to be fun. I shot him a wink that had him shaking his head good naturedly, then, a second later, I sent the cue ball sailing across the table. The crack rang out as it collided with the one, sending the rest of the balls flying. The twelve ball sank into the left corner pocket with a satisfying thud.

"Looks like you're solids," I stated as I straightened and moved around the table, looking for my next shot.

"Lucky shot," he muttered, but I could hear the underlying humor in his tone.

I narrowed my eyes in a quick glare before leaning back over the table. The way the balls were laid out, shooting with my dominant right hand would have been a little tricky, so I quickly switched to my left, lined up my shot, and sent my ball into the right side pocket.

He shook his head in disbelief, the corner of his mouth giving another tremble. I was getting closer. I could feel it.

"Luck has nothing to do with it. You know my family. A line of con artists and grifters as long as ours, we can hustle at pretty much anything." I gave him my most doe-eyed smile, the one I used every time I hustled someone at pool or poker. "If we were playing cards, I'd own your house and your car by now."

I was gearing up for my next shot when he chuckled,

and the unexpected shock at hearing that deep, husky sound had me shooting wide and missing my ball entirely.

I looked up to find the tiniest smirk possible tugging at his mouth. Somehow that teeny, barely-there curve of his lips was sexier than any smile from any other man on the planet. Unfortunately, it was gone so fast that, had I not caught it when I did, I might have thought it was just a figment of my imagination.

He moved around the table like he hadn't just let a flicker of emotion pass through the walls he seemed to keep firmly in place. I shook it off and headed for the small high-top table in the corner where we'd put our drinks. I sipped my wine as he rounded the pool table, looking for a move. I noticed the slightest hitch in his gate as he moved, something that a normal person who hadn't been trained to read expressions and body language as a job would have missed completely, but was more focused on ogling.

My gaze traveled down slowly, taking him in while I had an unobstructed view and a chance to stare without being obvious. His jeans looked faded and soft, like they'd been washed a million times. They hugged a firm round behind that was downright biteable, and strong, tree-trunk thighs. His button-down encased powerful arms, a wide chest, and broad shoulders. He radiated power with every move, every breath. It was a beautiful thing to watch. I never would have thought I'd use the word beautiful to describe a man like Hunter, someone so rugged and manly, but that's what he was to me.

He took his shot, sinking one of the solid-colored balls

into the pocket. He gave me a smug look before moving on and sinking his next shot.

"Not bad," I said with a grin as he lined up his next move. "You're good. But I'm better."

He gazed up at me from his bent position, one brow cocking. "That so?"

"Yep," I answered with all the confidence in the world.

"Care to put some money on that?"

I shook my head on a chuckle. "Sorry, honey. I can't take your money like that."

He missed and I moved back to the table to take his place. "I noticed you've been hired on here. Stella said you were making the move to Hope Valley permanent. How's the town treating you?"

I lifted my eyes after by ball slid into its pocket with a thud. If I hadn't been damn good at this game, the shock at the number of words that just passed his lips might have caused me to miss. "Well, holy shit. Did Hunter McCann just initiate a conversation? Quick! Look out the window and tell me if the sky is falling, would you?"

He rolled his eyes and took a pull from his beer. "Just take your shot already, smart-ass."

I did, sinking another ball as I began to explain, "Hope Valley's been great so far. Rory's an amazing boss and the people are a lot nicer than I'm used to."

I could feel his probing gaze as I studied the table for my next play. "People weren't nice to you in the city?"

I let out a breath, took my shot, and missed. I stood tall, sending up a silent curse at missing such an easy move.

When I lifted my eyes, Hunter's gaze was firmly on me, as though he were waiting for a response before he carried on with the game.

"It wasn't that they weren't nice, exactly."

"Then what was it?" he pressed.

"Well, I just . . . I couldn't exactly let people in, given what my family did, you know? Not that many would want in," I added on a grumble.

"Did you like what you did?"

My chin jerked back at the question. It wasn't something many people asked. They'd form their own conclusions, but they didn't come right out and ask, especially so bluntly.

"You're asking if I liked letting gross, cheating assholes feel up on me while I played at wanting them in order to steal from them?"

His expression remained completely neutral. "That's what I asked, yeah."

"No," I said flatly. "I freaking hated it. Best thing to ever happen was West falling for Stella. It didn't just get her out of the life, it got all of us out. Some people might not think waiting tables at the local watering hole is glamorous, but this is the best job I've ever had."

He didn't say a word as he bent back toward the table and resumed the game, the expressionless mask he wore never once budging. Finally, after sinking his next two shots, he looked up at me. "As far as those people not wanting in are concerned, fuck 'em. You did what you did for your family. Anyone who doesn't get that isn't worth your time. And this job's honest work. Not a damn thing wrong with that."

"Nope, not a thing," I said with a smile.

The man might not give a single thing away, but at least he seemed to understand me. And that was more than I could ask from most people.

Four
Serenity

As it turned out, Hunter was a better pool player than I'd given him credit for. As the hours ticked by, we played one game after another. After the fourth, we were tied, two to two.

I was just about to recommend one last tiebreaker when my sister came skip-wobbling over to me, looping her arm around my waist and swaying heavily into my side. "There you are! I've been looking *everywhere* for you."

I wrenched my head back and blinked rapidly, the alcohol fumes coming off her breath burning my eyes. "Was I at the bottom of that barrel of wine you drank?"

Stella giggled uncontrollably as she attempted to shift into a sloppy two-armed hug. "You're so funny." She teetered back around, her hair whipping so fast it slapped me in the face before getting caught in my lipstick. "She's not just gorgeous," she announced to whoever was close enough to hear, which meant Hunter and West. My cheeks began to burn. "She's also *suuuper* funny. And smart! She's gorgeous and funny and smart! My big sister." She tipped her face up to me, her eyes trailing a few seconds behind. I was sure the look she was attempting to give me was supposed to be affectionate or something, but she was so drunk she was cross-eyed.

I turned my wide eyes at West. "If you were hoping for some drunk sex tonight, you missed the mark about three drinks ago."

He skillfully extracted me from his fiancée's anaconda grip and twisted her so she was pressed up against him. "It wasn't even that many. You know what a lightweight your sister is."

He wasn't wrong about that.

"We were just coming over to say goodnight."

At his words, I shifted my attention over his shoulder to find that the bar had started clearing out at some point without us even noticing.

"Oh wow. I didn't realize how late it was." I'd been having such a good time with Hunter that the night had totally gotten away from me.

"Yeah, I need to get her home before she passes out on the floor. We'll see you at family dinner on Sunday?"

"Of course." I lifted onto my tippy toes to press a kiss to his cheek, and when I pulled back, I noticed Stella was currently passed out against him, her mouth hanging open, little chuffing snores popping out. I curled my lips between my teeth to keep from laughing. "Get her home safe, yeah?"

He hoisted my sister up like she weighed next to nothing. "I will, promise."

"And make sure to turn the volume all the way up on her phone and put it really close to her head so she can hear it when I call at the crack of dawn."

He shook his head on a chuckle. "Only if you don't sell me out."

I let out a long laugh. "Don't tell Spence, but you're officially my favorite brother."

He kissed my cheek before giving Hunter a chin lift and heading out, carrying my sister's dead weight.

"Guess that means it's time to call it a night," Hunter said, once we were alone.

I pasted a smile on my face to hide the disappointment causing my stomach to sink. I wasn't ready for our night to end.

"Yep. Guess so."

He took the pool cue from my hand and replaced it and his on the rack hanging against the back wall. "Come, on. I'll walk you out."

"Oh, you don't have to—"

Those Arctic eyes pinned me in place with a stony look that sent a tremor through my body. "It's late and dark as hell outside. I'm walking you to your car. That's not up for debate."

I ignored the tiny thrill that ran through me and rolled my eyes at his bossiness as I grabbed my purse and looped the strap over my shoulder. "Fine. But only because you asked so nicely," I chided.

He let out a noise as I started past him that could have been the start of a chuckle or just another of his signature grunts. Like so many other things about him, it was impossible to tell.

Together, we started toward the door. When Hunter's large hand came to rest on the small of my back, I had to bite my cheek to hold my shiver at bay. Heat instantly radiated from his palm up my spine and throughout my entire body, lighting me up like a Christmas tree.

"Night, Sere. See you next shift," Mona called.

"Yeah." The word came out on a croak. I cleared my throat so the rest of my sentence sounded halfway normal. "Goodnight, sweetie. See you soon."

He held the door open for me, surprising me once more with just how ingrained his manners seemed to be.

"Would you look at that?" I teased with a twang as I stepped past him and out of the bar. "Who knew you was so chivalrous under all that grunting and brooding."

That corner of his mouth trembled again as he mumbled, "smart-ass." I was wearing him down. I just knew it. It was only a matter of time.

The chilly night air was fresh with the smell of the pine trees that stretched tall along the craggy mountains surrounding the town.

I stopped beside my car and pulled the invigorating air into my lungs as I looked up at the sky. The stars glowed by the millions. It was as if someone had flung white paint against a black wall.

"God, I'd never seen so many stars until I moved here. I

could stand here for hours and stare up at them. Don't they just take your breath away?"

"I've never really noticed before."

Hunter's voice came out even gruffer than normal, pulling my focus from the stars. He wasn't looking at the night sky. His attention was solely on me. Even though the darkness swallowing up the parking lot cast shadows across his face, I could feel the intensity radiating off him when our eyes connected. It made all the air whoosh from my lungs.

His gaze was like a physical touch that I felt in every fiber of my body.

My heart began to beat staccato against my ribs, playing them like a xylophone as my lips parted and I pulled that fragrant air inside. My voice came out quiet and breathy, almost a whisper, as I said, "You should always make time to look up at the stars."

I could have sworn he shifted closer. "Yeah?" he rasped out. "Why is that?"

"Because while the world keeps spinning and things keep changing, those are the one constant. If you ever feel like the rug has been pulled out from under you, all you have to do is look up and somehow that awe-inspiring beauty makes everything feel just a little bit better."

I knew I wasn't imagining it when he moved in that time, because the rich smell of the pines was muddled by something spicy and manly and all Hunter. His glacier eyes shimmered in the dull parking lot light, pulling me into his orbit. If there was one thing I knew, it was when a man wanted me, and despite the mask that made him nearly impossible to read, in that moment, there wasn't a single doubt in my mind that Hunter was feeling the same thing I was.

"I had a lot of fun with you tonight," I said, continuing to speak in a hushed tone.

"Me too, Wildcat."

Without a single thought to what I was doing, I closed the last bit of distance between us and lifted onto the tips of my toes so I could get closer. Wrapping an arm around his neck, I pulled him down for the kiss I'd been fantasizing about for weeks.

I felt a sizzle the moment our lips touched that bloomed and grew, spreading through my entire body. However, that heat started to dwindle when I felt Hunter's frame go completely rigid against mine.

I was just about to pull back when something inside of him snapped. One hand came up to fist in my hair at the same time he looped his arm around my waist and yanked me against him.

Where I'd started soft, Hunter plundered, shoving his tongue past my lips to stroke and tangle with mine. I tasted the bitterness of the beer he'd been drinking earlier mixed subtly with the mint of his toothpaste. It wasn't a combination that should have been appealing, but on him, it was ambrosia.

His fingers clenched tighter in my hair, pulling my head back so he could take the kiss even deeper. A faint sting radiated through my scalp, driving me absolutely crazy. It was just enough to send a rush of arousal through my blood before centering between my thighs. All he'd done was kiss me—hell, the man hadn't even copped a feel —but it was still enough that I felt pressure building deep in my belly.

"God," I moaned into his mouth as I reached around and dragged my fingernails down his back, bunching the material of his shirt in my hands, "you're even better at this than I imagined."

I wasn't sure what snapped him back to reality, but one moment I was in Hunter's arms, the only place I'd wanted to be since the first time we met, and the next, his fingers were wrapped around my upper arms and he was shoving me away from him like my touch had burned his flesh.

"What—" I started on a pant, my breathing labored like I'd just run a marathon, but the rest of the words died on my tongue when I blinked my eyes back into focus and saw the expression on Hunter's face. It took me a moment to place what I was seeing, mainly because I'd never had a man look at me like that before. He looked both feral and haunted at the same time.

"Hunter. Are you okay?" I asked, reaching out for him.

"That shouldn't have happened," he clipped so harshly my hand froze in midair before dropping back to my side.

My stomach plummeted so fast it was a wonder it didn't make a crashing sound as it landed at my feet. "What?"

"That was a mistake," he said in a tone devoid of all emotion. "It won't happen again."

I shook my head, trying to force the pieces into place so what was happening made sense. I knew what I saw, what I felt. He'd wanted the kiss just as badly as I did, and once the shock wore off, he'd been all in. I hadn't imagined that. "I don't understand. That wasn't just me. You kissed me back."

"I shouldn't have." He let out a thready breath as he reached up to rake a hand through his dark hair, sending it into disarray. "Look, Serenity, I think you're great," he started, causing a sense of dread to swell in my stomach like a rock. Nothing good ever started like that.

Then he lowered the hammer. "But nothing is ever going to happen between us. I'm sorry, but I'm not the guy you're looking for, trust me."

He didn't say another word or give me a chance to object before he spun on the heel of his boot and stomped off into the shadows. I stood frozen in place for well over a minute, my mind reeling, before the thunderous rumble of a motorcycle engine jolted me out of my daze. Moments later, Hunter whizzed past, and I was left standing all alone in a dimly lit parking lot, feeling like I'd just been kicked in the ribs.

FIVE
HUNTER

I could feel the heat even from yards away. It penetrated my clothes and stung at my skin like thousands of angry wasps. The putrid smoke filled my lungs, the heavy musky scent choking out everything else. All I could smell was death and destruction. I stood there helpless, my chest in a vise grip as I watched the flames rise higher, the angry yellow and orange lashing up at the dark sky above.

The fire was a living, breathing thing, destroying the structure it like it was the enemy. Panic froze me to the spot, refusing to release me from its snare as I stared on, devastation eating away at me like the fire was eating everything before me.

Move, Hunter, the voice inside my head screamed. *There's still time. You can get them out. But you have to fucking* move!

My feet came unglued, taking me closer, but the heat

was overwhelming, hissing and spitting furiously. The closer I got, the worse my skin sizzled until I was forced to stop again. Tears of powerlessness poured from my eyes, the heat from the fire drying them into tight, salty tracks before they could make it all the way down my cheeks.

Then I heard it. "Bubby!" A voice, so scared, so tiny and innocent, that would haunt me for the rest of my life. "Bubby, where are you? Help me. *Please*!"

I shot awake to the voice ringing in my ears and the acrid smell of the fire in my lungs. The words became an echo that lingered before finally fading into silence. I pulled in a deep breath, the smoke and fire replaced with the salty tang of the sweat that coated my skin. My heart jackhammered against my breastbone, and despite the clamminess covering my body, I could swear I still felt the blistering flames on my flesh.

I flung the covers aside, feeling too constricted as I forced myself to calm my frantic breathing. I dropped my head back, thumping it against the wooden surface of the headboard once I was able to fill my lungs. I squeezed my eyes closed and reached up to pinch the bridge of my nose as the lingering effects of the nightmare slowly loosened their crippling hold on me.

It had been a while since one of my nightmares was so bad it woke me up in the midst of a full-blown panic attack. Those horrible dreams were a regular occurrence for me, given the *real* horrors I'd lived through. As sad as it was to admit, I'd grown used to them. Usually, I was better at shaking off the effects, but that wasn't the case tonight.

I was off my game, and there could only be one reason why.

That kiss with Serenity.

It had been fucking with my head since the moment my brain engaged enough to realize what the hell I'd been doing and put a stop to it.

I let out a sigh and shifted, throwing my legs over the side of the bed. I braced my elbows on my knees and scrubbed at my face and head, trying to scrub away the memory of that goddamn kiss. But it just wasn't happening.

I couldn't remember the last time, if ever, a kiss had gripped me so tightly and refused to let go. I hadn't been lying when I said I wasn't the man for her. I couldn't give her what she wanted, but that didn't mean one single kiss with Serenity hadn't rattled me so intensely that I was still feeling the vibrations all these hours later.

I'd fucked up tonight. I'd known it as it was happening, but it was as if I'd been standing outside my body, watching it happen and unable to do anything to stop it. I'd lowered my guard just enough for Serenity Ryan to sneak in while I wasn't looking.

If ever there was a woman who was off-limits, it was Serenity. Not only did I work with her sister, but Stella was marrying one of my Alpha Omega brothers. That made Stella Ryan family, and by association, Serenity as well. I had a reputation for being a man who'd never settle down, so if West thought for even a second that I was fucking around with his soon-to-be sister-in-law, he'd skin my ass alive.

And I'd deserve it.

A glance at the glowing white numbers on my alarm clock showed it was barely four in the morning, but after that nightmare, I knew there wasn't a chance in hell I'd be getting back to sleep.

With a weary sigh, I reached down and massaged the spot on my left leg where it had been amputated years ago, all thanks to an RPG in the middle of the desert in Afghanistan. The prosthetic leg I used was second nature by now, but even after all these years, the phantom pain was still there, aching and throbbing in a limb I no longer had.

That horrible day was just one of the causes of those nightmares that would plague me for the rest of my life.

Just like the nightmares, I pushed the pain to the back of my mind as I rolled the liner over my residual limb before sliding the prosthesis into place. I moved through my house, autopilot guiding my way, until I got to the kitchen and flipped the switch for the overhead lights. I headed directly to the coffee maker and set it to brew, then turned to rest my hips against the edge of the counter as I waited.

Something shimmery from the corner of my eye caught my attention, and I knew exactly what it was before I even turned to look. The invitation that had been slowly torturing me sat in the same place on my kitchen island that it had been in since I first opened it weeks ago.

The gold foil embossing caught beneath the pendant lights hanging above the island, sparkling happily while just the reminder of that goddamn piece of cardstock felt like a fist to the chest.

There was no fucking reason for that invitation to still be sitting where it was other than I must have had a masochistic streak a mile long. I already had every single word of that swirly, delicate font carved into my brain. I'd told myself a million times to just throw the fucker away, but I couldn't make myself do it.

Like every time I entered the kitchen, I moved over to it and read it again and again, twisting that knife in my gut just a little bit deeper.

Because you have shared in our lives
with your friendship and love, we,
Vera Moss
And
Oliver James
Request the honor of your presence at our wedding . . .

I stopped reading then, that fist in my chest growing tighter and tighter. I knew the date and time of the big day. I knew the address. I'd even looked up the fucking directions. I just had no intention of going.

I couldn't do it.

It had been bad enough, all those years ago, when I'd silently loved Vera from a distance as she and one of my best friends fell for each other. Craig Moss wasn't just a buddy. He was a brother in every sense of the word but blood. For as long as I could remember, it had been Craig, Glenn Danielson, Bryce Dixon, and me. We'd gone through training together and were in the same SEAL team. We'd seen action together, we'd bled together. That created a bond stronger than everything.

Craig and I had both seen her in that little dive bar in the middle of Nowhere, Arizona that night, but she'd picked him. And I never said a word. I had resigned myself to never speaking a word of my feelings out loud. I owed Craig my life, after all. He'd gotten me out of more scrapes than most people would get into in their lifetime.

There wasn't a single time when he hadn't had my back, so if he was lucky enough to win a woman as incredible as Vera, I would swallow down the pain, pin a smile on my face, and be happy for my brother that he was living the good life.

However, my leg wasn't the only thing I'd lost that day in the desert. When the smoke finally cleared and the dust settled, Bryce and I were the only ones who'd made it out of the rubble alive.

Losing Danielson and Moss was more painful than losing any goddamn limb. That was a pain that never went away. It felt like an eternity before I was finally released to go home. My career, the only thing I'd had worth anything, was over. My brothers were in the ground, and my body was ravaged.

By the time I made it to Vera, I was a nothing more than a broken shell of a man, but for all the pain and suffering I'd been dealing with, Vera's was acutely worse. Where I was a shell of a person, she was barely living.

I did my best to pick up whatever pieces I could, the pieces that shattered when Craig died. They'd had two small boys. Luke had only been four, Liam just two years old, when their father died, and the fact that they probably wouldn't have any memories of him, of one of the best men to ever grace the planet, tore at my very soul.

I did what I could for all of them. I was a male figure for the boys, trying my damnedest to teach them all the things I knew Craig had wanted to teach them. I was a shoulder for Vera to lean on. I was the one who made repairs around her house. The one who held her as she cried, night after night for what felt like an eternity.

The more time I spent with the Moss family, the more deeply engrained I became until I hadn't the first clue what my life looked like without them, who I was, or what I was meant to do. I depended on them more than I should have. The truth was, I was playing a role that wasn't mine, wearing a costume that didn't fit right. I wasn't their father. I wasn't her husband. As much as those boys had come to mean to me, and as in love with Vera as I was, I knew the stagnant life I'd forced myself into wasn't fair to any of us. Even knowing that, I'd been the chump who stayed, year after year, all because of hope.

Hope that was eventually dashed when Vera started to date.

Turned out, she needed me for pretty much every aspect of her life . . . except one.

That had been my breaking point. I'd put in a call to Bryce. That was when he told me about Hope Valley and Alpha Omega. He set up an interview a week later, and two days after that, I was starting over.

The years kept ticking by and I kept waiting for the day when I'd stop wanting her, but it never came. I'd spent so long trying to get her out of my head anyway I knew how. I'd drowned myself in work, buried myself in other women, but nothing worked. There was no one else but her. No matter how I tried to snuff out that need, every time I closed my eyes, it was Vera's face on the backs of my eyelids.

Until tonight.

With Serenity.

Vera had been the furthest thing from my mind while I had Serenity's soft, lush curves pressing into me. She'd fit against me perfectly, almost like she'd been made for me. Her skin had been so soft, her hair felt like silk, and she smelled like jasmine.

As I squeezed my eyes closed, there was nothing on the backs of my eyes. There was only the feel of the woman I was holding, the punch of lust her kiss brought on, setting my blood on fire. There was nothing in that moment but her, and it scared the living fuck out of me.

I wasn't supposed to feel like that. I didn't have it in me. After all the shit I'd lived through, I wasn't sure I could ever be the kind of guy *any* woman needed.

The gurgle of the coffee machine sounded, pulling me from my melancholy. Shaking off the black cloud I felt hovering over me, I filled a mug and carried it over to the sliding door that led to the deck. I needed fresh air as badly as I needed caffeine. My leg cramped up as I lowered myself into one of the Adirondack chairs that looked out at the view that had sold me on this house in the first place.

Normally, staring out at the forest and foothills that butted up to my property helped to calm my frayed nerves on bad days. Unfortunately, the shadows from the dark, moonless night had swallowed them up just then.

It was then that Serenity's words from earlier penetrated the dull, gray fog in my head.

"You should always make time to look up at the stars."

I threw back a gulp of coffee and rested my head on the back of my chair so I could stare up at the inky sky.

The inhale I'd just taken got lodged in my throat. She'd been right. Every thought, every worry, that had been plaguing me suddenly seemed so small, so damn trivial, as I focused on those millions and millions of glowing specks of light peppering the sky.

At least for the moment, I was able to let everything else go and think only about the beauty in front of me.

What Serenity Ryan didn't know was that she'd given me a gift just then. She gave me peace. Unfortunately, I knew I'd never be able to pay that back.

Six
Serenity

"Hey, honey. You good?"

At Rory's question, I looked up from my task of rolling silverware in napkins to find my boss had come out from behind the bar, leaving one of the other bartenders to handle restocking the fridges back there, and had taken a seat across from where I was working.

The Tap Room might have been a bar, but it also served lunch and dinner, so it was open most of the day and well into the night. Tips on the day shift weren't quite as good as when people were feeling boozy and loose with their purse strings, but since the cook rocked a pretty killer menu during daylight hours, there was a steady flow of patrons from the time the place opened at eleven in the morning until close.

I blinked "Huh?"

"You've been really quiet this morning. In fact, you've

been quiet the past few days," Rory pointed out. "I know you haven't been here long, but that doesn't seem like you. Everything good?"

I thought I'd done a decent job of covering the pouty mood I'd been in since Hunter shot me down three days earlier, but apparently, I thought wrong. Since he took off on his motorcycle, I'd been in a funk that left me feeling uncomfortable and itchy, and no matter how hard I'd tried, I hadn't been able to shake it.

I'd given myself countless pep talks over the past few days, determined to shake the melancholy off. He was just a man, after all. Nothing worth getting myself all tied up in knots over. Only, as much as I repeated that mantra, there was a voice in the back of my head calling me a liar.

It was that voice that reminded me of all the things that drew me to that man in the first place, the connection I felt to him, like we were kindred in some way.

I lowered my head back to the work I'd been doing. Mindless as it was, it kept my hands busy, never a bad thing. "I don't know what you're talking about." I offered her a smile to press the point home. "I'm great. Just a little tired, I guess. Still trying to get used to the late hours."

"If you need more days and less nights, just let me know," she offered without missing a beat. "I try to be as accommodating to my staff as possible."

My smile grew more genuine as I reached across the table and gave her hand a squeeze. I couldn't have asked for a better boss than Rory Paulson. She had a heart bigger than the entire state of Virginia and it showed daily, and not just with how she treated those of us who worked for her.

A few years back, a boy threw a rock through one of the bar's windows. When her man Cord caught up to the kid and brought him back, they discovered he'd been seriously abused while in the foster care system. She'd walked through fire, doing everything that needed to be done so Zach could live with her where she could keep him safe. Eventually, she and Cord adopted him, but knowing his wasn't the only horror story when it came to the foster system, she started a charitable foundation.

That foundation was responsible for creation of a group home right here in Hope Valley call Hope House. It provided kids in foster care a clean, safe, hell even *fun* place to live. The goal of everyone who worked at Hope House wasn't only to keep a roof over these kids' heads then put them out the door the moment they aged out, but to help them thrive in every single way possible.

That took heart, guts, and conviction. In the short weeks I'd known her, I respected her in a way I didn't many other people.

"No need," I answered her earlier question. "I like the lively crowd, and the tips don't hurt either," I added with a wink.

She chuckled and reached over to the stack of silverware and began rolling. "If you say so. But if anything ever changes, you let me know."

Like I said, best . . . boss . . . ever.

Just then, Fletcher shoved through the swinging door

that led from the back, carrying a bin of clean glasses. It was like it happened in slow motion. His long, lanky arms trembled under the weight of the heavy bin, his face was a strained shade of red, and his shoulders were hunched in an awkward position he couldn't possibly hold for much longer. He only made it two and a half steps from the kitchen when he finally lost his hold and sent the bin crashing to the floor.

I shot from my chair and started in his direction, Rory on my heels, just as the boy shouted, "Son of a bitch!" and dropped to his knees.

He was in the process of cleaning up the shattered glass with his hands when I rounded the counter and crouched down to his level.

"Here, let me help."

"It's fine. I've got it," he grunted. In the short time he'd been working here, surly grunting and clipped, snide remarks had been his constant choice of communication.

Fletcher had been one of Hope House's most recent charges, a seventeen-year-old boy who had a chip on his shoulder the size of Rhode Island. He'd only been there for a few months, removed from his own home by the state when his eighteenth birthday came and went. The director of Hope House, a woman by the name of Tessa, had insisted he stay, worried he wasn't quite ready to be on his own just yet.

Rory agreed, fearing that if they put him out, he'd end up right back where he'd started. As a way to help him start building a life, she'd hired him on as a busboy at the

Tap Room, hoping to teach him responsibility, as well as put some money in his pocket.

"You can't clean this mess with your hands." I circled one of his boney wrists with my fingers when he moved to grab a large, jagged piece of glass. "You're going to hurt yourself."

He snatched his arm back like my touch had burned him, his forehead pinched in a severe frown. "I don't need your help. I'm not a freaking baby."

I braced my hands on my knees and shot him a warning look. "First of all, that's not the tone you use with someone who's trying to help you out." I paused, giving him time to respond. When he said nothing, I cocked an eyebrow and rested back on my haunches so I could cross my arms. "Is it?"

He kept his eyes downcast and his voice in a low mumble, as he responded, "No."

"No what," I pressed, channeling my own mother. We might not have had the most conventional upbringing, but my mom never tolerated disrespect.

"No, ma'am," he said on another grunt.

I nodded my head in approval, just like my mom would have. "All right. Now go grab a broom and dustpan from the back and I'll help you get the rest of this picked up."

Rory lowered herself down beside me once Fletcher disappeared through the door to the back, and together we pulled the glasses that were still salvageable from the bin and moved them to the side. "Sorry if I stepped on your toes there," I said. "I probably should have let you handle that, huh?"

"No. You did great."

My brows rose high on my forehead. "Really? I mean, I know he's been through a lot, and I probably could have been a little nicer—"

She stopped me with a shake of her head. "You're right, he's been through a lot and picked up some serious baggage along the way, but part of helping these kids is having a firm hand with them. If we just gave them their way with anything or let them run rough shod over us, we'd be doing them a disservice. One of the main things almost all of the kids who come to Hope House need to learn is that there is such a thing as discipline and authority without cruelty. You were right in demanding he treat you how you deserved to be treated, and you did it without being cruel. I have to say, that's a gift. Not everyone has the patience or wherewithal to keep their cool."

My forehead pulled into a frown as I stared off at where I'd last seen Fletcher. My heart gave a little tug as I thought about what a kid his age had to have suffered through to make him so unhappy. It wasn't right, and it wasn't fair. He deserved something good, even if he remained a grumpy grunter for the rest of his life.

I was about to ask Rory what exactly it was Fletcher had been through when the kid shoved through the door once again, broom and dustpan in hand.

I shoved up without another word and carried the

glasses that were still intact to the guy manning the dish-washer just off the kitchen.

My face pulled into a wince as I sat the glasses he'd only *just* washed down in front of him. "Sorry, Frank. Hate to double your work, but we had a little accident out front."

He waved me off with a jovial grin. "Stuff like that happens. I'll have these out for you in a jiff."

I skipped over to him and placed a loud, smacking kiss against his ruddy, weathered cheek. "You're the best."

"Don't I know it, doll," he said on a laugh as I headed back to the front of the bar and got back to work. Without any more accidents, we quickly got into the flow of things. I moved on autopilot as I finished prepping to open. I was so focused on the task at hand that I hadn't noticed all other work had stopped as I moved through the bar, lifting the chairs off the tables and tucking them into place.

The sensation of eyes on me, that prickling of the skin on the back of your neck, alerted me to the fact I had an audience and pulled me out of the zone I'd been in.

I stopped with one of the chairs hanging midair, self-consciousness swamping me as I looked around the bar and noticed that Rory, Fletcher, Dan, the bartender, and one of the waitresses, Tammy, were all staring at me. "Uh . . . What? Am I in the middle of a wardrobe malfunc-tion or something?" I looked down at myself, then spun in a circle in an attempt to check my ass.

"Damn, woman," Dan said as he dried a glass with a hand towel. "Who knew you had a set of pipes like that."

My brows dipped in confusion. "Huh?"

"You've been singing along with the juke box." Rory's smile was so big it looked almost painful.

"I was?" I tended to do that. If there was a song playing that I liked, I'd sing along mindlessly, not even realizing I was doing it.

"Uh, *yeah*, babe," Tammy replied. "And your voice is *amazing*!"

Rory nodded enthusiastically. "It really is. You sounded incredible. Why didn't I know you could sing?"

My cheeks heated at being the center of attention. I shrugged. "I don't know. Why would you know something like that? I'm just a waitress."

"Girl, that's sacrilege," Tammy insisted. "Voice like yours, you should be front and center on a stage." She stopped and sucked in a gasp so big you'd have thought an A-list celebrity had just walked in and asked her to carry his baby. "Oh my God! I know what you should do. You should totally sing on Friday when the Makin Hardware Guys come in to play."

A few times a month, the Tap Room hosted a live band. A group of men who worked at Makin Hardware played together, and it just so happened that they were damn good musicians. Much better than they were at naming themselves, that was for sure. But there was no way in hell I'd get up on stage and sing.

"Yeah, that's never going to happen," I stated firmly as I lowered the chair the rest of the way to the ground and moved on to the next.

"Oh, come on," Rory said, joining in with Tammy like

this was the best idea they'd ever had. "But you're so good! You should totally do it."

"Not happening." I stopped what I was doing and turned to face them, my hands planted firmly on my hips. "The only place I sing is alone in the shower, and that's how I plan to leave it."

Tammy, known as the fun, boisterous one around the Tap Room, poked her bottom lip out in a pout. "You're no fun."

"No, I'm not." I shot her a wink as I moved past her. Taking the hand towel I had tucked into the ties of the apron wrapped around my waist, I spun it in the air before popping her in the backside with it as I passed her on my way to the back. "And don't you ever forget it."

SEVEN
HUNTER

Pushing through the door of Muffin Top, the smell of roasted coffee beans was an instant hit to my senses. I was in desperate need of caffeine after another shitty night of sleep. The nightmares had been coming with regularity now. For the past week and a half, I hadn't been able to get more than four or five hours a night, and I was beginning to feel it.

Fortunately, the best coffee shop in the country was nestled right here in my little valley.

"Good morning. Welcome to Muffin Top," the owner, Danika, greeted automatically at the chime over the door as I stepped inside. Her smiling face was a welcomed sight as she looked up from the customer she was helping. It was how she greeted each and every one of her patrons, and part of what made this place as successful as it was. She made everyone feel welcome, as if they were her favorite customer.

I tipped my chin up in greeting and tacked myself onto the line that was at least seven people deep, praying that it would move quickly. Normally it didn't matter when I made it into the office. Our boss, Lincoln Sheppard, wasn't the type to enforce office hours or micro-manage. As long as we didn't fuck off and got our work done in a timely manner, he let us be. But one of the women at Alpha Omega, Sage Caine, had taken it upon herself to make a coffee schedule, and today was my day to pick up drinks for the office. And if I was late I risked being the target of her temper, something no human being on the planet wanted to be subject to.

It was terrifying how someone so tiny could have such attitude.

The line shuffled forward just as a soft, melodic laugh floated back from the counter and hit my ears. It was a laugh I'd heard plenty of times in the past month or so since she'd entered my orbit, but it never failed to make my body tighten. It had the most beautiful musical quality to it.

It was a laugh that felt like a sucker punch to the gut after a week and a half of not hearing it because I'd been avoiding Serenity Ryan and the Tap Room like my life depended on it. Instead, I'd gone home night after night and stared at that goddamn invitation until my eyes began to cross. Then I'd move outside and stare up at the stars. It was a vicious cycle.

I might not have seen her in person the past several

days, but that kiss was still burned onto my brain, and no matter how hard I tried, I hadn't been able to get Serenity out of my mind.

I felt myself leaning to the side for a better look at the front of the line. Sure enough, there she was. Her back was to me, but I recognized that long sun-kissed hair that hung down her back like a sheet of gold.

Her shapely body was showcased in a pair of jeans and a tee that nipped in at her waist, enhancing her hourglass figure.

It was no wonder she'd been so damn good at running honey pot cons on men for her family. The woman had looks that could knock the breath right out of your lungs. When she smiled it was always full out and uninhibited, making her hazel eyes sparkle. There was a natural flush to the apples of her cheeks that was highlighted by a delicate nose and defined cheekbones. Then there was her body.

I'd seen her dressed down as she was just then, and I'd seen her after pulling out all the stops for a night out. She could go from pin-up to sweet girl-next-door without much effort, and since she started working at the Tap Room, it had become impossible not to notice the way men's eyes seemed to gravitate to her like a tractor beam.

The thing that threw me off though, was that she didn't seem to notice. Given what she and her family had been known for, I'd expected her to play it up whenever she worked the bar, but she wasn't doing that. Most nights, all that golden straw hair was pulled up in a messy bun at the top of her head to keep it out of her way. If she wore any makeup—not that she needed it—it was always the bare minimum. Her jeans were just tight enough, not painted on like some of the other waitresses looking to thicken tips, and she rocked the standard Tap Room T-shirts just like everyone else.

I'd be the first to admit that I'd made a snap judgement upon meeting Serenity Ryan, and I'd been dead wrong. After the night of her sister's engagement party, I knew that beyond a shadow of a doubt.

Spending those hours with her, just the two of us, I'd gotten more than a glimpse of her personality. She was quick to joke and just as quick to laugh. She gave out those show-stopper smiles without hesitation. I learned there was so much more to her than the wrapping. She was clever as hell, cunning, smart. She was funny and nearly impossible to embarrass because she was the first to crack a joke at her own expense if it was warranted.

She was passionate, kind, and loyal to a fault. There wasn't anything she wouldn't do for her family. The love she held for them was inspiring.

She said something that made Danika and the other barista behind the counter throw their heads back in laughter before picking up her paper to-go cup and giving them both a wave before she turned to leave.

The minute she completed her twist, those bewitching eyes landed directly on me. My stomach sank as she stutter-stepped in her boots and the smile fell from her face at the sight of me. I felt like the world's biggest asshole, but before I could react or issue an apology for how I'd left her the other night, I watched in fascination as she shored up her resolve right there in the middle of the coffee shop.

She shook off the hesitation that had hit her when she first spotted me. Squaring her shoulders, she pinned another smile—this one only slightly less brilliant—and started in my direction.

That was another thing I'd learned about Serenity that night. The woman had more courage in her little finger than most men had in their entire bodies. Where I'd taken the route of a chicken shit, avoiding her after an awkward encounter, it was obvious she was going to brush what had happened aside and move past it.

She stopped a few feet away, her fragrance, that subtle jasmine scent, just strong enough for me to catch over the smell of coffee and sugar.

"Hi," she said without missing a beat.

"Hey, Wildcat."

"You having a good morning?"

I felt the corner of my mouth tremble. This woman was something else. "I will be just as soon as I make it to the front of the line and have a cup of coffee in hand."

She giggled as she lifted her own cup, the sound like chiming bells. "I feel that. I wasn't much of a coffee drinker until I moved here, but this place has turned me into an addict."

The tension in my shoulders slowly started to melt

away. She was making this a hell of a lot easier than I deserved. "Well, welcome to the club, Serenity. We meet every morning between the hours of seven and ten in the morning. Then again around three PM."

That earned me another smile. "Sere," she said in return, giving me a moment of confusion.

"Huh?"

"Sere. Kind of like 'hey Siri, start my get-funky playlist.' It's what my friends call me, and I figure there's no reason we can't be friends, right?"

A chuckle worked its way up my chest, the vibration rolling past my throat. "I don't see any reason why not. Even though you have a playlist titled Get Funky."

"Hey, don't knock the playlist, man. I fire that thing up, and I guarantee, even a broody bastard like you couldn't hesitate moving to the beat."

"Highly unlikely."

Her brows raised in challenge. "Want to bet?"

That was a lesson I'd learned the night of the engagement party. Those three words were dangerous coming out of her mouth. "Not a chance in hell. I learned never to bet you when we were playing pool."

She reached out casual as could be and gave my chest a reaffirming pat. "Don't sell yourself short. You held your own, buddy. If I remember correctly, we ended the night tied, two-two."

Technically, we ended the night with her wrapped around me like I was a tree she wanted to climb and my dick trying to bust through the zipper of my jeans, but I kept that thought to myself.

She looked at the watch on her wrist and suddenly started to move away from me, walking backward as she said, "I need to get going, but it was nice running into you."

"Same, sweetheart," I said, actually meaning it.

She gave me a look, one corner of her mouth quirking up in a crooked smirk. "Does that mean you'll stop avoiding the bar now that we broke through the awkward?" she asked, calling me on my shit without missing a single beat.

I couldn't help it, I laughed full-on. "Yeah, Sere, that's what it means."

She hit me with that beaming grin I get in my gut. "Great. Then I'll see you tonight," she said before turning on her boots and pushing her way out of the coffee shop and onto the sidewalk. It wasn't a suggestion or even a question. That was her not-so-subtle way of telling me I'd be going to the Tap Room tonight, simply because she said so.

I finally made it to the front of the line and put in my order, feeling a hell of a lot better than I had when I first woke up this morning. My mood had picked up considerably by the time I made it into the office—with just two minutes to spare to avoid the eruption of Mount St. Sage.

I passed out the coffees before grabbing my own and heading toward my office. I'd just taken my first sip, the dark, rich flavor of the brew sparking on my tongue before traveling down and giving me that much needed hit I'd been looking for when my cell started to ring.

I reached to pull it out of my back pocket and smiled at the name on the screen. I swiped to answer as I rounded my desk and kicked the chair out so I could sit.

"Shouldn't you be in class right about now?"

I heard a huff come through the line, then a familiar voice dripping with teenage attitude. "Jeez, Uncle Hunt, I'm walking there right now. I have a few minutes before class starts, so I thought I'd call you."

It might have been several years since I moved away from Luke and Liam after realizing I needed to build a life of my own that wasn't centered around their mother, but that didn't mean I hadn't kept up with them since I'd been gone.

Those boys were probably the closest I'd ever get to having kids of my own. I might not have been their father, but I hadn't been able to stop loving them like they were my own flesh and blood. Nothing would ever change that. No matter what happened with Vera, I'd make sure my boys never lost me.

"Glad you did. Always good to hear your voice. How are things? You still seeing that same girl you told me about a couple weeks ago?"

"Nah. Cammie dumped me when I showed up five minutes late to pick her up for a date, even though it was because I got a flat. I'm talking to a new girl now. Rebecca. She's cool."

"That's good, bud. You making sure you treat her right? Show her respect?"

That earned me another huff and a groaned, "Yes, Uncle Hunt."

"Good man." I'd started calling Luke a man a couple years back. It always made his chest puff out with pride when I said it, and I loved giving him that. Only, this was the first time it hit me that it was getting closer and closer to being the truth.

It seemed like it was just yesterday he was a lanky, knobby-kneed kid. Now he was sixteen—nearly seventeen —driving around in his own car and dating his way through high school. It was amazing the things that made you feel old as hell.

"So, how's everything else? How's Liam?" I stopped to swallow down the wad of cotton that was drying out my throat. "How's your mom doing?"

"Liam's fine, I guess, when he's not annoying the shit out of me."

My voice dropped with a warning. "Hey, watch it. For one, I doubt your mom likes you using that language. And two, I don't care how annoying you think he is, that's your brother, and he's the only brother you've got. I don't want to hear you talking about him like that again. You got me? You two need to learn to get along and have each other's backs."

"Sorry, Uncle Hunt," Luke said sullenly. "You're right."

"Remember that. It'll do you good in the future."

I could hear the smile in his voice as he said, "Yes sir." Then his mood shifted with his next topic. "Actually, I'm calling you because of Mom."

My stomach plummeted like I was on a steep drop on the world's highest roller coaster and my heart began to beat like I'd just run up a steep hill at a dead sprint. "Is everything okay? Did something happen?"

"No, no," he said quickly, reading the urgency and worry in my tone. "It's not like that. It's just, well, she was talking to me last night about the wedding and stuff, and she mentioned that you hadn't RSVPed. She asked if I'd talked to you about whether you were coming or not. I told her we hadn't, but I got the feeling she was bummed out that maybe you weren't planning on coming."

Squeezing my eyes closed, I leaned back in my chair as far as it would go while pinching the bridge of my nose. This was a conversation I'd prayed I wouldn't have to have. The boys didn't know the real reason I'd left to move to Hope Valley. They were too young and didn't need to know the dirty details of it all. As far as I knew, Vera hadn't told them either. The last thing I wanted to do was lie to either of them, but the truth could potentially put a wedge between us, and I just couldn't let that happen.

"Yeah, buddy. Tell her I'm sorry about that. I've been looking at my schedule here at work," *lie*, "and I just don't think I'll be able to swing it," *lie*. "I wish I could be there," *biggest lie of all*, "but it's not looking good."

"Oh, okay." The dejection in his voice ripped my insides to shreds. I hated myself for lying to him, but more,

I hated that I was the one to make him feel anything but good. I just couldn't stand it.

I clenched my fist until my knuckles turned white and ground my molars so hard it was a wonder they didn't crumble to dust. "But you know what?" I found myself saying before I could stop the words. "I'll see what I can do."

Just like that, the happy, easy-going Luke I knew was back, excitement brimming in his voice. "Really?"

"Yeah, pal. I'll make it work."

"That's awesome, Uncle Hunt! I just haven't seen you in a while, you know?" I did know. I tried to get to them at least once a month. I'd take a couple days off work to make a long weekend, and travel down to them in North Carolina. I'd take them hunting or camping or fishing, something that was just for us guys. But it had been hard to find the time to get down there the past couple of months. Then I got the wedding invitation.

"I know, bud. I'm sorry for that."

"Liam's gonna flip. This is awesome. I can't wait to see you."

Jesus, but the kid was undoing me. I'd just fucked myself, and there was nothing that could be done to fix it. It would mean letting Luke and Liam down, and I couldn't do that. I just couldn't.

"Me neither. Tell your mom I'll get that RSVP to her soon, yeah."

"Yeah, you got it. Hey, the bell just rang, I need to get to class."

"All right. I'll see you soon. I love you."

"Back at you. And soon."

With that, the call disconnected, and the bright mood I'd been experiencing since my earlier run-in with Serenity disappeared in a puff of smoke.

EIGHT
SERENITY

I t was Friday night at the Tap Room, and thanks to the live band on stage, the place was a mad crush of people. It was barely 9:00, but my feet were already killing me from being run ragged, trying to keep up with all my tables.

But the cash in my apron was steadily growing fatter by the minute, meaning I'd probably be able to buy those incredible strappy heels I spotted in the window at a local boutique sooner than anticipated.

Silver lining.

The energy in the bar was electric, dosing me with a much-needed burst of adrenaline every few minutes. The music was pumping, the band was killing it. But the main thing that kept me going was the fact that every table I stopped at held a familiar face that didn't hesitate to offer a greeting, like I was a long-time friend. Ralph and Sally Hanson, the couple who ran Evergreen diner, chatted with me for a quick minute after I'd taken their order, insisting that I come in soon for lunch. Joe Silvester, the kindly, weathered man somewhere in his seventies or eighties had taken a beat to flirt with me as I delivered him another pint.

I was quickly becoming engrained in the fabric of Hope Valley. And it felt incredible. I loved my family like crazy, don't get me wrong. But it was nice to have people outside of that circle. It was nice to be looked at without judgement. I finally felt like I belonged, and I couldn't find the words to describe how that felt

The only person who wasn't friendly was a woman by the name of Sue Ellen Mayfield, but I'd been warned about her before my very first shift. According to rumor, she was just an all-around miserable person who tried to lift herself up by picking apart everyone around her. From what I could gather, she wasn't a town favorite, but that hadn't stopped her from acting like her shit didn't stink.

I'd had a couple run-ins with her already, and she hadn't failed to show her claws. It had to suck, leading such a miserable life. I almost felt sorry for her. *Almost*. She was just too horrible of a person to garner my sympathy.

"Here you go, Mitch," I said as I placed an IPA in front of the old man. He was sitting with Joe and a couple of other guys. Apparently, they played cards together on a regular basis and ran as a pack. All I knew was they were sweet as hell, unrepentant flirts, and tipped well.

"You're an angel, Sere girl," Mitch said with a smile, the lines on his face carving even deeper as he gave me a wonky smile that creased his papery cheeks. "If I was just half a decade younger."

I placed my hand on his knobby shoulder and gave it an affectionate squeeze. "If you were half a decade younger, I don't think I'd survive you."

The table broke out into hoots of laughter, and I bent to place a kiss on Mitch's shiny bald head before moving off to check the rest of my tables.

Movement from the corner of my eye caught my attention, and I turned to find my sister's arm in the air, waving wildly to get my attention.

My face stretched into a wide smile, and I started in her direction as I scanned her table. Of course, West was there, but so was Bryce Dixon, another AO hottie, and his lovely wife, Tessa. Lincoln Sheppard, Stella's new boss, and his wife, Eden, an adorable doe-eyed woman with the thickest, most beautiful hair I'd ever seen, were there too, as well as Marco Castillo and his wife, Gypsy. The last couple circling the table was Sage and Xander Caine. Sage worked at Alpha Omega as well. That was where she'd met the mountain of a man she eventually married. If I thought Hunter was the strong, silent type, he had nothing on Xander. With his size, his hard features, and damn near constant silence, he might have been downright scary. But I'd seen the way he looked at his wife like she hung the moon. I'd also seen how the tiny sprite of a woman fought with him when she was feeling feisty. Any man who could handle a spitfire like Sage was all right in my book.

If the Alpha Omega crew was in tonight, that meant

Cord was there as well, probably at the bar, hitting on his wife. I chanced a quick glance to the bar, and sure enough, he was planted on a barstool, leaned over with his hand at the base of Rory's neck so he could pull her closer for a kiss. I'd met them all here and there, and I'd come to like each and every one of them.

Then my eyes reached the end of the table. And there he was. Rounding out the group was none other than Hunter McCann. A thrill shot through my veins at the sight of him, but I quickly tamped it down. He'd made it perfectly clear how he felt—or didn't feel, to be precise—about me, and as much as it stung, I'd been determined to move past it.

After a week and a half of him avoiding me like I was Typhoid Mary, we'd reached a somewhat reluctant truce earlier that morning. Friendship wasn't exactly what I'd been hoping for, but I'd made my move and lost. My pride was still stinging, but I had to move on.

Friendship was better than nothing, right?

Or at least that was what I kept telling myself. There was still that insane draw I felt to him, like a tether that kept us cinched together somehow. I couldn't bring myself to ignore it, which was why I'd felt the need to lead us to a common ground we could both be okay with.

For some strange reason, I felt like there was a reason we were in each other's lives. That something stronger had a hand in us meeting.

Stella hopped up the moment I reached the table and wrapped me in a hug that I quickly returned.

"I didn't know you were coming in. If you'd told me I would have held a table for you guys closer to the stage."

She waved me off. "We wanted to sit in your section. Besides, it was last minute. Hunter said he was coming in for a beer, then I remembered there was a band tonight."

I looked back to Hunter. When I'd issued my challenge at Muffin Top earlier, I hadn't thought he'd actually bite, but here he was.

Like the heat in my blood, I pushed that thought down. Being here didn't mean anything other than he was taking our attempt at friendship seriously. If he could do it, so could I. I wasn't going to be that woman who read into every tiny little thing until I turned it into something it wasn't. He'd made his position clear, and I was determined to take him at his word, no matter what.

I dipped my chin to him in silent acknowledgment before the rest of the table. "Well, if you're in my section, you better tip well. I've been eyeing a pair of stilettos in a shop window off Main, and tonight is the night I make them mine," I teased, drawing a laugh from most everyone.

"Ooh! The ones at Glitter and Gold?" Sage asked with a little hop in her seat. "I've seen those. You've got great taste, babe. That place is awesome. That's where I got these." She extended a leg out from under the table to show me the pair of gray studded ankle boots she was rocking. They were killer, and I wanted them instantly.

"I *love* those!"

She twirled her foot in a circle before dancing it from

side to side. "Right? They're the best. You get those heels in the window and we can trade off now and then."

Man, but the people in this town were *awesome*! "Deal," I agreed, then I got down to business, because I needed those tips more than ever. "What can I start you guys off with?"

I scribbled their orders down on my notepad and headed for the bar where Rory and Cord were still going at it like they were teenagers, not a married couple with a teenager who should have grown sick of each other long before now.

"Think you two can quit sucking face long enough to fill this order? I've got tips to earn." I waggled my eyebrows when they broke apart to look at me. "Momma needs a new pair of shoes. Literally. If I don't get them, I'll throw a conniption to end all conniptions."

Cord let out a pained groan as Rory giggled and move from him to take my ticket. "I'm on it."

I shot Cord a wink in response to the playful glare he was throwing me. "Oh relax. You already know she's going home with you. She's a sure thing."

"Don't I know it," he said with a smirk before lifting his pint of Guinness to me in salute and heading over to the table I'd just left to join the rest of his crew for a bit.

I turned from him to scan my section as I waited for my drinks, mentally taking note of who I needed to check next, which tables to clear, and who needed refills, when I felt someone move up beside me.

"Hey gorgeous. Buy you a drink?"

I looked over to a man who'd pushed his way through the crowd to sidle up into my personal space.

I gave the man a small grin that probably looked just as forced as it felt. "Sorry, pal. I'm on the clock." I pointed to my name tag and the T-shirt that read, "I Make an Art of Tapping That." Those tees were just one of the many reasons I loved working here. Each one said something different, all dripping with sexual innuendo and funny as hell.

The guy crowding me against the bar looked at me in a way that made my skin crawl. His grin was one I'd seen far too often in my other life, one that said he was an entitled prick who didn't know how to quit while he was ahead.

"Then how about you take your fifteen-minute break, we go out back, and I show you a good time?"

I looked him up and down, my expression flat. "But then what am I supposed to do with the remaining eleven minutes?"

His chin jerked back in bewilderment. He hadn't been expecting that, and if I didn't think he'd read into it the wrong way, I would have smiled at my win.

Before he could figure out what to say next, I put him out of his misery. "I'm not interested. Not sure there's a woman in this place who would be with a proposition like that. Work on your game and try it on someone else. But I suggest you don't come right out of the gate trying to get in their pants."

Rory's timing was impeccable. She plunked my drinks down on the bar in front of me, and I quickly loaded them on the tray without giving the asshole another look or thought.

With the tray balanced on one hand, I moved through the throng of people until I hit Stella's table. I passed out drinks and was about to move on when a hand on my wrist stopped me.

Tiny sparks of electricity lit beneath my skin like miniature lightning bolts, traveling up my arm and expanding in my chest as I looked down to where Hunter was touching me, holding my in place.

I slowly exhaled as I lifted my gaze to his. His brow was creased in a deep frown as he asked, "You okay?"

My head tilted to the side in confusion. "Of course. Why?"

"That guy at the bar. The one who was in your face. It looked like he was bothering you."

I sucked in such a big breath my lungs threatened to burst like balloons. I let it out slowly, silently willing the squealing voice inside my head to shut the hell up. It wanted to believe Hunter had been watching me close enough to notice that guy meant something more than it really did.

He hadn't been watching me, I told myself. He wasn't tracking my every move. Odds were, he'd looked around the bar and just happened to catch the scene as it played out. That was all.

I pulled my wrist from his grip, my skin, once heated, suddenly going cold at his lack of touch. I waved him off like it was nothing. "Oh, that was no big deal. I'm used to it. It's nothing."

He didn't look any happier or reassured. "Not something you should have to get used to, Wildcat," he grunted.

Oh, if only that were true. It was something that he, as a man, would never understand. "Sadly, it comes with being a woman. You're right, I shouldn't have to get used to it, but until society somehow teaches all the pigs and assholes out there to treat women with the respect we're owed, we have to deal with shit like this on a regular basis."

My comment only seemed to make him unhappier, and the way his eyes traveled back toward the bar to where the man from earlier still stood, nursing his drink, sent a shiver down my spine.

"I don't know what that look on your face means, but I don't like it," I said in a warning tone. Leaning down, I lowered my voice. "Whatever you're thinking, Hunter McCann, knock it off. Starting a bar brawl isn't going to do *anyone* any favors."

He looked like he wanted to argue, but eventually pulled in a deep breath and nodded in agreement.

The relief I felt at dodging that bullet was short-lived, however, because a second later, the singer on stage was saying my name, along with a lot of other words that made my lungs seize and the blood in my body turn to ice.

"A little birdie told us that one of the Tap Room's newest family members has a set of pipes on her that'll bring the house down. Ladies and gentlemen, please give a huge round of applause to Serenity Ryan!" The crowd burst into applause and the man behind the microphone talked over them. "Serenity, get your bee-hind up here and joins us for this next song."

"What?" I squeaked as my head began to shake frantically. "No way. No, no, no."

My wide, crazed eyes spun back toward the bar, specifically, to Rory and Tammy, the so-called little birdies, both cheering wildly and shooting me thumbs-up.

I was going to freaking kill them!

Nine
Serenity

The fire I was shooting from my eyes did nothing to quell the excitement coming off those two as they began chanting my name. I was going to get my revenge. I didn't know when, and I didn't know how, but I'd do it, damn it.

Stella stood up and whooped loudly, her arms in the air. "Come on, Sere! Sing for us," she shouted at the top of her lungs.

I was still shaking my head—a lot of damn good it was doing me—as hands from different patrons began pushing and guiding me toward the stage. I wasn't getting out of this. Everyone was going to make sure of that.

I moved woodenly toward the stage, feeling like I was trudging through cement. The lights felt blinding as I climbed up the single step that took me onto the platform.

"Come on, darlin'," the lead singer coaxed gently, leaning in to speak closer to my ear. "You'll get used to it in no time." I wasn't so sure about that. It felt like it was a million degrees hotter up here than it was on the floor. "You know what you want to sing?"

Did I know? Of course I didn't know! I wasn't even supposed to be up here. "Uh . . ."

"What's the last song you listened to?" he asked, guiding me toward my choice.

I remembered the last song I'd queued up on my phone and sang along to as I cleaned my tiny apartment earlier that day. "Do you know 'Lighthouse' by William Prince?"

He grinned big and nodded. "Mic's all yours, sweetheart."

I took place front and center as he informed the rest of the guys in the band what song they'd be playing. Before I was ready, the music swelled and the crowd went quiet. Fortunately, the gentle, calm melody filled me up. I closed my eyes against the lights and people and transported myself right back to my living room. I was all alone, singing for myself, not a packed bar. Feeling a sudden peace wash over me, I let the words flow past my lips.

———

Hunter

"My God, Stella. Your sister has the most incredible voice," I heard Gypsy exclaim from farther down the table.

I heard mutters of agreement from the rest of the crew at our table, but I couldn't pull my eyes off the woman standing behind the mic, her long, delicate fingers wrapped around the stand. She gently swayed side to side, unconsciously, as she sang. Everything about Serenity in that moment was mesmerizing.

I understood now why her laugh always affected me the way it did and why it reminded me of music. It was because she'd been hiding this gift. There was a quality to her voice I hadn't expected, a smoky huskiness, like the smoothest hit of whiskey sliding down your throat. It was sexy and sultry, not high like something you'd expect to hear on one of those cartoon princess movies. It was dark and moody, like rich chocolate.

"I love when she sings," I could hear Stella saying from the other end of the table as my attention split in two, one half listening to her, the other entranced by her older sister's bluesy, hypnotic voice. "She could be famous. I don't have a single doubt about that. I've told her a million times that if she just tried, she could really go places."

"Why doesn't she?" Sage asked.

From the corner of my eye, I saw Stella shrug. "She doesn't want it. She's always said she just wants a normal, happy life. Being a star was never appealing for her."

A normal life, I thought to myself. I wasn't sure there were many people out there who wouldn't jump at the chance to be famous if it was presented to them. It was interesting to know Serenity Ryan wasn't one of them. I was quickly coming to realize that there were layers to the woman I'd never expected. She was so different than I'd originally thought. She was an onion you could keep peeling and never reach the center.

It was intriguing as hell.

Not that it mattered.

The song reached its crescendo and Serenity's voice rose higher, hitting notes that had the crowd inside the Tap Room going nuts, before finally drifting back down quietly as she closed out the song.

As soon as the last note faded, people shot to their feet, clapping and whistling and whooping for the incredible performance put on by the gorgeous woman on stage.

Her cheeks were flushed a rosy pink as she laughed awkwardly and covered them with her hands. "Thanks. Thank you," she stuttered into the mic and waved nervously. "I appreciate it, but I'm handing it back over to the professionals."

Kyle Makin, the guy who fronted the local band, returned to the microphone and pulled Serenity into a hug that made my muscles tighten inexplicably. *Get your shit together,* I silently chided myself. *There's nothing between you and her, and there never will be.*

I knew the jealousy churning in gut at the platonic hug was ridiculous, but I couldn't help but think back to that kiss we'd shared just a few yards from here, right outside. It had thrown my whole world off balance, and as hard as I tried, I still hadn't managed to right myself fully.

The hug finally broke apart, and he lifted her hand in the air as he spoke into the microphone. "Give it up one more time for the lovely Serenity Ryan, folks. Wasn't she incredible?"

The noise swelled again, and I watched her like a hawk as she moved off the stage and headed toward the bar, stopping every few feet when someone wanted to praise her performance. The smile that stretched across her face was so big it was damn near blinding as she took the time to show genuine gratitude to each and every one of them.

Wanting to be close to her, but needing an excuse, I sucked back the rest of my beer and stood. "Need a refill," I said to no one in particular.

"I'm sure Sere will be over any minute," Stella said.

I gave her a casual shrug. "It's no big deal." And I had no intension of waiting, no matter how long or short a time it was.

It was easy enough to get through the thick crowd. When a man my size was moving through, people tended to clear out of the way quickly enough. I was only a few feet away when I had to stop and cut a glare at the man standing closest to her at the bar. All he was doing was waiting to order a drink, but he was in my way.

He caught my look and quickly scampered off, clearing the space beside Serenity so I could fit into it.

"If I thought for one moment that I could get away with it, I'd murder you both so hard for that," I heard Serenity say to Rory and another one of the Tap Room's waitresses. Apparently they were the ones behind the ploy to get Serenity on stage.

"You were awesome, doll!" the woman in a "Tap it

Real Good" shirt stated. "You should be thanking us. And don't think for a second that's the last time you're getting your pretty little ass up on that stage."

Serenity let out a growl that sounded cute as hell as she snatched up a tray and tucked it under her arm. "You're lucky I need to see to my tables, or I'd practice trying to make your head explode with my mind."

She spun around, spotting me for the first time, and sucked in a gasp. I was close enough to see her pupils dilate and smell the jasmine on her skin, and not for the first time, I was hit with a thought that it was a shame I was a broken shell of a man, because a woman like Serenity deserved so much better than me.

———

Serenity

I couldn't believe Hunter had managed to get that close without me noticing. Usually, I felt his presence like a physical caress, a tingle that started at the base of my neck and worked its way down my spine like fingertips dragging across my skin.

It had to have been the adrenaline dump still working its way through my bloodstream that had come with singing in front of the entire bar that had clouded my mind to his sudden closeness, but now that I knew he was there, every inch of me became aware of him.

The manly spice of his blocked out all other smells, and I could practically feel the heat radiating off him.

I was going to have to get used to pushing down that initial punch of lust I felt every time I caught sight of him. I could only hope it would eventually go away for good. "Hi." I looked down and noticed the empty glass in his hand. "I'm sorry; you need a refill. I'll get right on that."

He shook his head to stop me as I started to lift my hand to catch the bartender's attention. "Don't worry about that. I just wanted to tell you it was damn impressive what you did up there, Wildcat."

I felt the nervous heat I'd only *just* gotten control of return to my cheeks. My chin dipped as I tucked a few loose strands of hair behind my ear and muttered, "Thanks. It wasn't exactly planned."

"Then I guess we're all lucky we showed up tonight."

I gave him a teasing scowl and poked at his chest. There was no give whatsoever to the firmness of his pec, and my mind instantly fell ass over elbow into the gutter. I couldn't stop wondering what he looked like without his shirt, or any of his clothes, for that matter.

I bet it was a work of art beneath all those clothes, not that I'd ever get to find out.

Damn it!

"I wouldn't say it was luck that got you here tonight. More like a friend pulling your head out of your ass."

The word *friend* might have tasted bitter on my tongue, but I'd get used to it. I'd say it over and over again if that was what it took to remind myself. Because that was all we were.

Cue internal pout and poor-poor-pitiful-me whine.

He smirked, and damn but he made that smirk look good. Everything from the perfectly grown scruff on his face to the creases in the corner of his icy eyes. A smirk like his was the best kind of lady porn.

"True enough," he conceded. "Guess my friend's a whole lot smarter than I am."

I grinned. "And don't you forget it. Now leave the glass and go sit back down. I'll be at your table soon with refills."

He gave me a salute before moving away from the bar and returning to his table. As hard as it was, I forced myself to get back to work. Even if I wasn't able to banish thoughts of Hunter from my mind, there was no reason I couldn't be productive.

Think of the shoes, I reminded myself, focusing on something else I wanted and would actually be able to have.

I managed to find my groove and worked the rest of my shift without a hitch. It helped that I wasn't forced to sing another song, but I could reluctantly admit—to myself only—that the performance seemed to have made a difference with my tips, because I ended up closing the night out with more cash than I'd ever made on a Friday night.

And I had to say, I hadn't *hated* it. Once the nerves

had dwindled, I actually enjoyed myself. It had been fun, and who knew? Maybe I'd do it again some time.

Last call came and went, and the bar steadily emptied out. I helped Tammy, Rory, Mona, and Dan close things up for the night, and by the time I stepped out into the brisk, black night, I knew I'd be out as soon as my head hit the pillow.

I called out my goodnights and headed toward my car parked behind the building in the staff lot.

I beeped the locks and reached for my door handle just as a strange, twitching sensation spread across my neck and down my arms, like someone was watching me. It wasn't like the awareness I felt with Hunter, however.

This feeling was darker, less thrilling, almost ominous.

I paused with my hand on the door and did a scan of the parking lot. There he was. Just outside the lot, standing on the sidewalk beneath a dingy pool of light cast by the streetlamp. There was a good bit of distance between us, so I didn't have the best view, but I could make him out just enough to know two things: first, I didn't recognize him, and second, he creeped me out in a very major way.

He wasn't doing anything wrong, exactly, just standing there on public property. But the way he was watching me left me all sorts of unsettled.

I didn't know what his deal was, and I had zero intention of sticking around to find out.

Yanking the door open, I climbed into the car and automatically engaged the locks. The music I'd been listening to on the way to work earlier blared to life as I cranked the engine, and in a matter of seconds, I was pulling out of the lot and heading toward my apartment.

It didn't take long for thoughts of the stranger to be snuffed out by thoughts of Hunter, and by the time I'd washed my face and brushed my teeth, the weirdo outside the bar wasn't even a memory.

Because I went to sleep and dreamed of the same man I'd been dreaming of for weeks.

TEN

SERENITY

I was back on the day shift a few days after the night of my reluctant performance. It was the first time I'd worked a shift with Fletcher since Rory had given me the tiniest bit of his backstory, and I found myself watching him closely as we prepped to open, my brain swimming with a million different questions.

I still didn't know the full story, but knowing what I did now, my heart cracked a little more every time I looked at him.

"I don't know what your deal is, but you need to knock it off," Rory hissed from behind me, jerking my attention from the hallway Fletcher had just disappeared down so he could grab a case of beer. "You're watching that poor boy so closely, I'm afraid he's going to come to me to file a harassment claim."

Okay, I had to admit that I was probably coming off a little creepy, but I couldn't help it. "I'm just worried about him. He's so closed off. It's like he's carrying the weight of the world on his shoulders."

She gave me a look of sympathy and reached out to give my forearm a comforting squeeze. "To him, it probably feels like he is."

"What happened to him, Rory?"

She let out a reluctant sigh before casting her gaze toward the hall that led to the stockroom.

"Come on." As if deciding it was too risky to have the conversation out in the open, she grabbed my arm and pulled me to the back and into her office, closing the door firmly behind us.

"Damn, is it that bad?"

She nodded. "Yeah. It's bad. Normally, the state wouldn't bother pulling a seventeen-year-old from their home. It's a sad, disgusting fact, but it's a fact nonetheless."

"So if they felt it necessary to intervene, it had to have been pretty damn bad."

She nodded solemnly. "It was. He grew up, just him and his dad, in a place up in the mountains. There's a group of people up there, doomsday preppers and the like, convinced the world is going straight to hell at an alarming rate. Most of them don't usually cause a lot of problems, mainly they're just determined to live the self-sufficient lifestyle. They don't bother anyone else and appreciate if we do the same, but there's a small offshoot that thinks our laws don't apply to them. It's mainly men, think their children and women are meant to wait on them hand and foot, cater to them. And they enforce those rules with iron fists. Literally."

Oh God, poor Fletcher.

I felt my blood start to heat, boil in my veins. "Let me guess, his father's one of those assholes, and his mom decided she couldn't handle it anymore and just left him to that hell all by himself."

She lifted a single shoulder in a shrug. "No one knows what happened to his mom. One day she was there, the next she wasn't."

I didn't think it was possible for my heart to hurt for him any more than it already did.

"That's all I know. Well, that, and the fact that whatever his piece-of-shit father put him through, nearly broke him."

I let out a sigh, my heart feeling heavy. "I'm almost sorry I asked."

"Almost?"

"Yeah, almost. Because if I didn't know, as much as it breaks my freaking heart, I wouldn't know what to do or how to act to help him put himself back together."

Rory blinked. Then smiled, *huge*.

"Why are you smiling like that? You look like something out of a scary movie."

"I'm smiling because you get it. Not many people do. The more people who know, the more we can help these kids."

She looped her arm through mine and led me out of the office.

The bell above the door rang just as Rory and I stepped back out front. I stutter-stepped before jerking to a stop at the sight of the man who'd just walked in. There was something vaguely familiar about him, but I wasn't sure where I'd seen him before.

The vibe that was pouring off him sent a chill through the air. A tremor worked its way down my spine the moment his eyes finished their scan of the bar and landed on me. There was nothing behind those eyes. They were like dark, blank voids.

"Sorry, but we're not open yet," Rory stated, trepidation reading clear in her tone. When I looked over at her, I saw her eyeing the man in a way that told me she felt the same thing I had. This was not a good man. "You're welcome to come back at eleven but for now, you'll have to go."

The man's eyes changed in that very instant. They were no longer empty, but full of so much hatred it caused me to suck in a gasp. Recognition took hold just then, and I remembered where I'd seen this guy before. He was the one standing on the sidewalk and staring at me the other night when I was leaving the bar.

"Don't take orders from the likes of you, heathen."

Rory rocked back on the heel of her kickass cowboy boot at the venom spitting from his words, but I had an altogether different reaction. The impact of the hate in his eyes dwindled at my own rising anger. Who the hell was this man to think he had any right to come into Rory's own establishment and talk to her like that?

"You need to leave, now. And don't bother coming back once we're open."

His focus shifted to me, his top lip curling up in a snarl. "I see you're the kind of woman who needs to learn her place."

I harrumphed at his audacity. "And let me guess, you're just the asshole to teach me, right? I seriously doubt that. Now, get the hell out, before I call the cops."

The man snorted derisively. "You think I'm gonna listen to some filthy pig and whore woman? Your laws don't mean shit to me." This guy must have been one of the ones Rory had just told me about. I didn't think I'd actually meet one in the flesh, but now that he was standing right in front of me, I wished I hadn't.

The laugh the man let out just then would have chilled me to the bone had my rage not been burning. "I'm not leavin' here without my boy."

I opened my mouth to ask what boy he was talking about when a loud clatter wrenched through the air like a gunshot.

I whirled around to see Fletcher standing at the mouth of the hallway. The crash had come from the broom and dustpan he'd been carrying. He must have dropped them because his hands were visibly shaking, and his face had turned ashen.

"Fletcher?" I started, concern for him quickly drowning everything else out.

"Time to go, boy," the man snapped aggressively.

My head bounced between the two of them like I was

watching a tennis match. "Wait. He's your—you're his—"
My focus centered on Fletcher, his behavior suddenly
making a lot more sense. "This is your father?"

He blinked like he was coming out of some sort of
trance and looked at me, his eyes glassy with fear that set a
whole new fire in my veins. He looked so much younger
than his eighteen years just then. He was scared to death,
and something inside me roared to life, screaming and
clawing with the need to protect him from the very thing
that had put that look of abject terror on his face.

"Fletcher!" the man snapped, his voice cracking like a
whip. "Won't say it again. Get over here, now. We're
leavin'."

I moved then, putting myself between Fletcher and
this vile excuse of a human being. I looked back over my
shoulder, holding my hand out to stop him while doing
my best to look as reassuring as possible. "Fletcher, stay
where you are, buddy. Rory, can you call the cops to
remove this piece of filth?"

She already had her phone pressed to her ear as she
rushed to Fletcher and threw a protective arm over his
shoulders. "Already on it."

"The hell do you think you are, standin' between me
and my own boy?" the man boomed. "That's my own
flesh and blood. He does what *I* say! Not some whore who
works in this den of sin."

I whipped back around, shoving my finger in the
man's face. "Then you should have thought about that
and treated him as such instead of like he was some piece

of garbage whose sole purpose in life was to cater to you. You lost all rights to call yourself his father, you sanctimonious prick!"

"Serenity, don't—" Fletcher tried to warn, but it was too late.

His father moved in even closer, and I would have been a liar if I said he didn't scare the ever-loving shit out of me, but I'd be damned if I let it show. I was Serenity Ryan, for Christ's sake. I would not be cowed by any man, but *especially* this one.

"Someone needs to teach you a lesson," he hissed, spittle flying from his mouth.

"Better men than you have tried," I said through gritted teeth. "And every single one of them has failed."

He looked me up and down in a way that had me suppressing the shiver that wanted to skate over my entire body. "Think I know exactly what to do with that whore mouth of yours. Once I'm finished with you, you'll know your place good and well."

"Careful. You should know, I hit back. And when I do, I hit hard." Preferably with my car. I wanted him to hurt. I wanted him to pay for what he'd done to Fletcher.

Sirens sounded in the distance, alerting everyone to the impending police presence.

"Dad," Fletcher said, his voice quavering, "don't make this worse. Please just go."

The man looked to his son and curled his lip in disgust before spitting on the floor. Then he turned back to me and shoved his finger in my face. "This isn't over."

With that ominous warning hanging in the air, he turned and bounded through the door like the coward he was. He might have thought he was above our laws, but the chickenshit was still too much of a coward to tangle with the local PD.

I wasn't surprised in the least.

I turned back around to find that Fletcher's face was a sickly shade of white, like he'd just seen a ghost.

I moved in his direction quickly, taking hold of him by the arms and adopting a soothing tone. "Hey, it's okay. You're okay now. He's gone."

"You—you shouldn't have done that."

"It's okay," I assured him. "He's not going to get near you ever again."

Fletcher shook his head frantically, the fear in his eyes only growing stronger. "I'm not worried about me. I'm worried about you. You just painted a bullseye on the middle of your back."

I had to admit, that didn't sound great, and yeah, it might have freaked me out a little. But that asshole didn't know who I was. He didn't know where I lived, and he sure as hell didn't know that I'd claw his face to shreds if he tried anything.

"I'll be fine. I promise. You don't need to worry about me."

He didn't look convinced, but before I could get another word out, the door to the bar burst open, and two uniformed officers came waltzing in.

In my old life, the sight of cops was something I'd wanted to avoid at all costs.

It was crazy how things changed. Because now, instead of wanting to sneak out the back to avoid the law, I suddenly felt like everything was going to be okay.

ELEVEN
HUNTER

My phone had pinged with an incoming message a couple minutes ago, and I'd been staring down at the words on my screen since.

Liam: *Luke said you're coming to the wedding. Can't wait to see you, Uncle Hunt!*

Looked like Luke hadn't wasted time spreading word that I'd be down for a visit for their mom's wedding.

I was thrilled to be seeing the boys again, no doubt about it. But I'd have rather had my teeth ripped out with pliers than go to that wedding.

A knock on the opened door of my office jerked me from my haze and took my attention from my phone.

"Jesus, brother. Who the hell walked over your grave? You look like you've seen a ghost."

I let out a whoosh of air, feeling my entire body deflate with it. Bryce Dixon was the closest thing I had to a brother. We'd served together, we lost Danielson and Moss together. Together we'd grieved those losses, and the loss of the lives we'd lost with them, and we both had demons from those battles in the desert that no one could fully understand but us.

He was the only one who knew everything about me, and I did mean everything.

"Just got a text from Liam," I said before scrubbing at my face with both hands.

He moved fully into my office, taking one of the chairs on the other side of my desk. "Everything good?" He knew all about my love for those boys and the feelings I still had for their mother. He'd stayed in touch with them as well, only on a different level.

"Yeah, it's fine, I guess." I could feel the steady pulse of an impending headache behind my eyeballs. "But I got sucked into agreeing to go to the wedding."

He let a hiss out from between his teeth. "Fuck, man."

I pressed my fingers into my eyes, hoping the pressure would alleviate the thrumming inside my skull. "I just couldn't say no to Luke when he asked."

"You can't say no to any of them, that's always been the problem."

I opened my eyes and saw him shooting me a hard, knowing look. "Don't start," I warned him in a low growl. "I don't want to hear this shit again, man."

The muscle in his jaw ticked and his nostrils flared on a deep inhale. This was a fight we'd had more times than I cared to think about. One that had nearly cost us our friendship. I held my breath, silently praying he'd let it go, because I really wasn't in the fucking mood.

Finally, he held his hands up in surrender. "Fine, man. I'll drop it. Just answer me one thing. You sure about this?"

I hesitated a beat, unsure how to answer because I wasn't sure what the hell the answer was. "I don't know, man. Honestly. It'll probably be a fucking nightmare, but I'll get through it."

"Well, fortunately for you, you'll have me—and Tessa —at your back."

I let out a steady breath of relief knowing they'd be at the wedding as well. I knew he'd been invited, but there had been a sort of unspoken agreement between us to not bring up Vera's wedding, so I hadn't bothered asking if he was planning to go or not. It was good to know I wasn't going to have to suffer through the day alone.

Just then, commotion out in the hall caught our attention, and we glanced to the doorway just as Cord barreled past.

"Whoa, brother," I called out. "Where's the fire?"

He back-peddled and popped his head past the doorframe. "Just got off with Rory. Something's going down at the bar. Not sure what, but Serenity Ryan's apparently waded into the middle of it, and the cops have been called. They're on the way right now."

The tension that had been tying my shoulders into knots snapped as adrenaline surged into my bloodstream at the mention of Serenity's name.

Before I knew what I was doing, I was on my feet and charging around the desk. "I'm going with you," I clipped, earning bewildered looks from Bryce and Cord.

"Guess I'll tag along to see the show," I heard Bryce say, but I was already out the door and down the hall.

I didn't stop to consider how my sudden behavior might look to my friends. There wasn't much that got me on my feet and moving as fast as I just had. Sure, I reacted to serious situations appropriately, but usually those involved assholes with guns and penchants for violence. In this case, the police had it under control, so me reacting so strongly had to have seemed strange.

But when Cord said Serenity had gotten in the middle of something that was bad enough to warrant a police presence in the first place, I simply reacted.

"You wanna tell me what's going on?" Bryce asked as he pulled the passenger door of my truck closed and buckled himself into the seat. "It's not like you to go off half-cocked like this."

"Don't know what you're talking about," I grunted as I threw the truck in reverse and hit the gas.

The bar was only a few blocks from our offices. We easily could have walked it, but I wasn't willing to wait. I didn't know why, but I needed to see for myself that Serenity was okay, and like hell I was going to delay doing that.

"Bullshit you don't know what I'm talking about," Bryce muttered from beside me, but I ignored him, all too happy to let us lapse into silence until we pulled into the parking lot of the Tap Room.

A cruiser sat near the entrance, parked catty-cornered across three spots. The engine was still running and the lights were on. I parked in front of it, not giving a single damn if I was properly between the two white lines, and killed the ignition.

Cord, who'd been right on our tail, met us on the sidewalk, and the three of us shoved into the bar, one after the other.

I spotted Rory first. "I told you we had it under control and you didn't need to come," she said as Cord made his way to her while I scanned the mostly empty bar.

There was a boy who looked like he was skin and bones, somewhere in his teens, standing near the bar, one of the bolted-down stools supporting most of his weight. He looked like he could keel over at any moment. But it was the woman standing beside him, hovering in almost a protective, Momma Bear kind of way, her hand resting comfortingly on his arm, that drew me in that direction.

While the kid was as white as a sheet, Serenity looked no worse for the wear as she talked to one of the uniformed officers I recognized, a man by the name of Fred Duncan. In fact, she looked fierce, her free hand gesticulating wildly as she talked, her cheeks flushed. The relief at seeing she was all right was overwhelming, but I refused to think too hard about it, at least for the moment. There was time to freak the hell out about it later.

My feet carried me in her direction without a single

thought to what I was doing. As I grew closer, I could hear the anger in her voice. However, the moment she spotted me, her entire demeanor changed.

The anger melted away, replaced with shock. The pink tinge on her cheeks remained, growing slightly darker, and her full, rosy lips parted slightly. I wanted to pull her hair free from the messy knot on the top of her head and bury my fingers in it as I plundered her mouth.

Damn it, this was not the time to get hard.

"Hunter?" Her voice came out in a squeak. "What— what are you doing here?"

I didn't stop until I was right in front of her, barely a few inches separating us. Needing to make sure there wasn't anything I'd missed, I gently took her chin in hand and tilted her face side to side. When I was confident nothing was bruised or broken or injured, I grabbed her by the shoulders, unable to stop touching her now that I'd started, and crouched just enough to meet her eyes. "Are you okay? What the hell happened?"

"I . . . uh . . ."

When it became obvious she wasn't going to answer for herself, Fred filled me in on everything that had gone down. My company worked closely with the local PD on several cases and had a good relationship with every cop in the place. They came to us when their hands were tied by legal constraints. Knowing we operated in that gray area they tended to have to steer clear from.

I'd known Fred for years. Back in the day, the man had been a pain in the ass, a guy not many had much respect for. But after being the first on scene of a brutal murder a few years back, something in him changed. A switch had been flipped. Gone was the ego that some men developed when they started carrying a badge. He took his job seriously, and he was damn good at it.

"Man by the name of Cyrus Whitlock came in and caused a scene."

I looked to the boy Serenity still refused to move away from. He was watching me warily, as if he was conscious of my every move and had to keep his guard up. The kid looked like he had more baggage than his lanky shoulders could possibly carry. But I saw something else in his eyes, eyes that seemed much older than his years. Behind the fear and the cautiousness, there was a strength that I recognized all too well. It was the kind of strength that came after undeniable suffering. It said he'd seen far more than he ever should have, but that he hadn't let it break him.

"It was my father," he spoke in a voice much steadier and deeper than I would have expected. "He came in because he wants me to go back home."

I arched a brow, waiting for more, but Serenity chose that moment to cut in. "But that's not going to happen." Her voice was unwavering and resolute. "I swear, we won't let that happen."

The kid looked to her, his face pinched with an emotion I couldn't put my finger on. "You shouldn't have gotten involved," he said in a whip-cracking snap. "You should have just stayed the hell out of it."

Serenity's eyes narrowed as she planted her hands on

her hips. Total Momma Bear. "First of all, watch your damn tone," she scolded, and the first thought in my head was that she looked fucking adorable just then. "Second of all, I was just trying to help you—"

The kid surprised us all just then by shooting off the stool and whipping around to go toe-to-toe with Serenity. "I don't need your help," he barked out so loud that Serenity flinched back.

"Watch it," I growled.

Fear flashed in his eyes when I got between him and Serenity, but he quickly masked it with anger. "This isn't any of your business. Just stay out of it."

"You made it my business when you started disrespecting the woman who had your back."

"She shouldn't have done that," he insisted, his face falling for just a moment, long enough for me to catch a glimpse behind the wall of ice he'd erected and see what was truly bothering him. He was scared, not for himself, but for Serenity. "It wasn't her place."

Serenity popped her head around me, fire licking in those sweet hazel eyes of hers. "Well, someone's gotta do it," she insisted.

Christ. Adorable.

I held out my arm and guided her back as gently yet firmly as I could, biting the inside of my cheek to keep from laughing at the tiny growl that rumbled up her throat.

I turned my focus back on the kid, who couldn't have

been much older than Luke. Suddenly, I understood Serenity's protective instincts.

"Tell me what's got you so worried."

His chest rose and fell with fast, labored breathes, as though he'd just run a marathon. "She shouldn't have threatened him like she did. When he gets mad, he can't let things go. He's not going to forget about that, trust me."

My insides seized as I slowly turned my head to look at Serenity. She at least had the decency to look nervous as she chewed on her bottom lip and shifted from foot to foot.

"You threatened him?"

"Well, not *exactly*."

That pressure I'd felt in my head earlier had returned and was starting to grow. "Then how, *exactly*."

"It was more like baiting him." She slapped her hands on her hips once more, that defensive fire returning and heating her cheeks. "But in my defense, he came in here and started harassing Fletcher, scaring the shit out of him. I tried telling him to leave, but then he started in on how I needed to learn my place and he was above the law and yadda yadda yadda—"

The rest of her words were drowned out by the blood rushing through my ears as I turned back to Duncan. "Cyrus Whitlock. Who is he?"

I had a sinking feeling in my stomach that was justified when he answered, "It's what you're thinking," he started, reading the sudden tension in my body clear as day. "He's part of the prepper community, up in the mountains. One of the extremists."

"God *damnit*," I hissed violently before whipping around on Serenity. "You and I need to talk. Privately."

She opened her mouth to argue, but I wasn't having any of it.

"*Now.*"

TWELVE
SERENITY

I wasn't thrilled with the idea of leaving Fletcher alone while he was still so rattled, but when I tried to object, the fire Hunter nearly breathed as he snapped, "*Now*," sent a tremor through me that wasn't half as enjoyable as the usual tremor he elicited.

Before I could get a word in edgewise, he gripped me by the wrist and started pulling me down the hall toward the back office. He was moving at such a quick clip I had to skip-walk to keep up with his long-legged strides.

He used his hold on me to propel me into the office, then slammed the door behind him, closing us in a room together that felt way too small, given the energy pouring off the guy, making the air thick and muddy.

"What the fuck were you thinking?" he boomed. "You're new here, so you don't know about these people, Sere. They're bad, fucking news. You're supposed to stay the hell off their radar, not put yourself in the goddamn crosshairs of a man like that."

Something to know about me, I didn't do too well with being backed into a corner. When the need to defend myself ever arose, I usually came out of the gate swinging. That was just part of the reason I'd gone at Fletcher's father as strongly as I had.

Now that Hunter was in my face, voice raised, anger steaming from his ears, that fight instinct was strong as hell.

I closed the distance between us and drilled my finger into the solid wall of his chest. I had to take a moment to swallow down the punch of lust that came with touching him—I was pissed, not dead, for crying out loud—before I let him have it.

"I was thinking that boy out there hasn't had a single person in his corner in his entire freaking life," I lashed out, my voice bordering on shrill. "I was thinking he deserved to have someone who was willing to fight for him at least *once*. But mainly, I was thinking about how that stupid son of a bitch pissed me off by insinuating my place as a woman was somehow beneath him, therefore, I needed to back up and mind my own damn business.

"You don't know this about me, Hunter, but I don't handle it too well when men think they're somehow superior, simply because they have a dick. That asshole said I needed to be put in my place, so I put him in his, because no one, and I mean *no one,* has the right to treat another human being like he's treated his own flesh and blood. If you have a problem with that"—I lost a bit of my steam on that one, wondering exactly where I was going—"well, then, it's just your damn problem. And maybe we shouldn't be friends anymore."

Oops.

That last sentence had escaped before I could pull it back. I was really bad about that.

He stood there, staring at me as those icy eyes of his glinted like sun on a frozen lake. Finally, when the silence between us was almost too much to bear, he spoke.

"You finished?"

I inhaled deeply, giving that some thought. The red-hot anger I'd been feeling earlier had lowered to a gentle simmer. It was still there, only nowhere near as strong. "I got mad," I admitted in a much calmer, quieter voice. "I tend to react without thinking when I get mad. I just saw how Fletcher locked up at the sight of him, and kind of lost my mind."

He reached up, surprising me by pinching a loose strand of my hair between his thumb and index finger, giving it a feel before tucking it behind my ear. "I understand that. Probably more than you know. I don't call you Wildcat for nothing, sweetheart."

I chewed lightly on the corner of my mouth as a whole swarm of butterflies took flight in my belly. "Valid point."

"But those people, they're dangerous, Sere. That kid in there—" he paused, waiting for me to provide his name.

"Fletcher."

"Fletcher is right. You can't just go off half-cocked. Not with them."

I already knew that. My gut had told me when I'd gone head-to-head with the man in the middle of the bar. Alarm bells had been blaring in my head, telling me to cool it, but the instinct to protect Fletcher had drowned out all reason.

"I know," I admitted reluctantly. "But, Hunter, I'm not worried about me. Fletcher was taken from him when he was seventeen. He's eighteen now. Technically, he can do whatever he wants. I'm just worried that if his father gets to him, he'll be able to suck him back into that life, and that boy deserves so much better than that."

A sudden wave of desperation washed over me. "I know you guys charge crazy prices for what you do. I can't afford to pay you up front, but I'm good for installments, I swear."

The small space between his eyebrows creased in a frown. "What are you talking about."

"I want to hire you to go talk to that guy, you know, like, persuade him that it's in his best interest to leave Fletcher the hell alone or something. I mean, if that's even something you guys do. I'm not saying I want you to rough him up or anything. Just . . . scare him a little bit. Men like him are cowards."

Although, I had a feeling Hunter already knew that.

"Sere, it doesn't work like that," he started with a shake of his head.

"*Please*," I pleaded. I closed the distance between us,

not even noticing I'd reached out to fist the material of his shirt at his stomach until those haunting blue eyes traveled down to my hands. When he looked back at me, something was swimming in those frigid depths that made my insides shockingly warm. "He's got no one, Hunt. His mom abandoned him, his dad abused him, and everyone around him turned a blind eye. He deserves a shot at something good. If he can't get out from under that horrible man, that will never happen."

Hunter's hands came up, his long, thick fingers wrapping around my wrists, making them feel positively dainty. I thought for a moment that he was going to pull from my grip, but he didn't. He simply stood there, holding my eyes as he held my wrists in a gentle grip.

Heat spread from where he was touching me, sparking to life and spreading through my entire body like vines that had grown out of control. "Is that what you need to feel at ease?" he asked, the question—as well as the tender voice he asked it in—making the breath stutter in my lungs.

"Yes," I answered with complete honesty.

"And if I do this, you'll make sure to stay the hell away from this guy? No more confrontations, and if you happen to see him around, you call the police or me, and let us handle it?"

I nodded, hope blooming in my chest. "Yes, I swear," I spit out quickly before he could change his mind. "Yes. Just tell me how much it'll cost—"

He clenched his fingers, tightening his grip, while

shaking his head. "I'm not taking your money. I'm doing this on my own, away from the firm."

"I can't ask you to do that."

"You didn't ask. I chose to do it."

Oh man, this guy was dangerous. To my wellbeing, my sanity, and my libido. He was making it incredibly hard to remember we were only friends and that was all we'd ever be. I dropped my arms, forcing him to release the hold he still had on me so I could move away. I needed a clear head when dealing with this man or I'd be traveling the road straight into heartbreak.

"You're a good friend, Hunt," I said with a smile. "I can't tell you how much it means to me you'd be willing to do that."

He hit me with the smallest, barely-there grin. "Don't mention it, Wildcat. If it keeps you from putting yourself in harm's way, I'm happy to help."

I did my best to ignore the way he made my insides feel all soft and melty, but damn if he wasn't making it hard.

Who knew the broody guy with the haunted eyes and grunted answers had a whole other side to him?

I sure as hell didn't.

THIRTEEN
HUNTER

"You want to tell me where the hell we're going?" Bryce asked, once again buckled into the passenger seat of my truck.

"Just sit there and be quiet," I grunted as I turned onto a road that took us higher into the mountains. "As I recall, I didn't invite you in the first damn place."

He might have been a brother to me, but that didn't mean he didn't give me a headache on a daily basis. With a nosey streak that rivaled that of the blue hairs in our small town, Bryce could gossip with the best of them.

I'd come back to Alpha Omega just long enough to do a quick search on Cyrus Whitlock, coming up not only with his address, but his criminal history as well. There were several charges of criminal mischief, harassment, and even one for domestic abuse that was dropped when his wife recanted her statement. The last one was for endangerment of a child.

How the prick managed to skate by the legal system, his punishments the bare minimum, blew my mind. The man never even saw the inside of a prison cell for his crimes. Each time he walked away with a few fines and a couple slaps on the wrist.

I was loathe to admit it, but Serenity had been right. If that kid didn't get out from under his father's thumb, he'd never stand a goddamn chance.

After I got the information I needed, I started back out, telling Roxanne I'd be working remotely for the rest of the day and to call my cell if something came up that I needed to know about. Just as soon as I'd clicked my seatbelt into place, Bryce was throwing open my passenger door and climbing in beside me.

"Well, no, you didn't invite me because you're a curmudgeon-y dick who'd rather be alone than spend time in my *fantastic* company."

I took my eyes off the steep, tree-lined road just long enough to cut him a sidelong glower, not that it did much good. Bryce Dixon, notoriously happy, notoriously a pain in my ass, wasn't fazed by my threatening glares in the slightest.

"But if I hadn't come, you might have had some fun without me. Plus, I wouldn't have had the chance to ask you what's going on between you and Stella's sister."

"There's nothing going on between us," I said way too fast.

From the corner of my eye, I caught him looking at me like he thought I was full of shit.

"We're just friends," I added when his silence began to gnaw at me. "That's all."

"Sure, you are," he deadpanned. "That why you ran out of the office like your ass was on fire when you got word there was trouble at the bar?"

"Bryce," I said in a warning tone he didn't bother to heed.

"Or why you beelined right to her and acted like she was the only one who existed once we got there?"

A growl worked its way from my throat, and I clenched the steering wheel in a death grip, making the leather creak. "Drop it. Before I pull over and kick your ass out of my truck so you have to walk back to town."

"Christ, Hunt. It's not like it would be the end of the world if you did have feelings for her, man. She's a good woman."

"I'm very aware of that, man." More than aware. I knew exactly how good she was, and it was better than the likes of me deserved. She was sunshine. I was darkness. The two didn't belong together. She was just trying to start a new life for herself. She didn't need my bullshit baggage weighing her down. "Now let it go."

He let out a gravelly huff, and I knew him well enough to know he desperately wanted to keep going, wanted to pound his logic into my head until it finally stuck.

However, we both knew that wasn't going to happen.

The rest of the ride to Whitlock's place was made in blessed silence. A few minutes later, I took the turn onto a poorly maintained path. If I hadn't been looking for it, I would have missed it completely. It was more mud than gravel, ruddy and covered in potholes that were big enough to rip the undercarriage off a smaller car.

No Trespassing signs were hung on every other tree, the verbiage growing increasingly more threatening the farther along we drove.

"What is this place?" Bryce asked, leaning forward in his seat. "Some sort of hillbilly hell?"

He wasn't too far off the mark, but before I could answer, the lane came to an end just before a large cluster of mobile houses and RVs. This was some sort of ramshackle compound formed by the offshoot of the prepper community up here in the mountains, the ones known for causing trouble.

I knew from my research that Cyrus lived in the single wide trailer that was in such bad shape, it looked like a stiff breeze—or not even so stiff—would send the whole thing crashing to the ground.

There was a dog chained to a dead tree in the dirt patch acting as a pitiful front yard, his snarled, foaming barks surprisingly vicious given the fact I could count every one of his ribs from thirty yards away.

"Jesus Christ, I was right," Bryce said under his breath. "This place is hillbilly hell. Where the fuck are—?" He clamped his mouth shut, realization dawning. "Have you lost your mind?" he barked, whipping around in his seat to look at me. "You were going to come out here alone? Are you fucking crazy? You know what these doomsday nut jobs are like."

I was fully aware.

I pulled to a stop closest to the house I was looking for and threw my truck into park, twisting my neck to look at Bryce. "You want to sit here bitching at me, or you want to have my back while I take care of something?"

"What the hell could you possibly have to handle out here? I haven't heard of a single case coming through AO that deals with these people."

"This isn't work. This is personal."

His brows shot up. "For who?"

There wasn't a chance in hell that I would tell him the actual truth. That Serenity had clutched onto me, that jasmine filling my nose and those worried sea-colored eyes gripping my insides as she asked me to do this.

Not. A. Chance.

"That kid from the bar," I started to explain. "This is his father's place. If you can call that piece of shit a father. I'm just paying him a friendly visit to stress the point that he needs to stay up here on his mountain and the fuck away from the kid and my town."

"Fucking hell," he tucked his chin and massaged his forehead. It took him a few seconds, but just like I expected, he got on board. "All right, fine. But I swear to God, if this goes south, I'm getting my revenge in the form of babysitting duty. That means you're responsible for feeding and dirty diapers, and *your* eyelid will be the one that's pulled back so he can scream into it."

Bryce and Tessa's son, Dillon, was about eight months old now, and while I loved the kid and thought he was the shit, I had no desire to deal with any of the things Bryce had just mentioned.

"Let's just get this over with so you can get home to your eye-screaming kiddo, yeah?"

I killed the engine, and the two of us climbed out of the truck. Our drive up the lane hadn't gone unnoticed. Doors had opened and people had started pouring out onto front stoops. But it wasn't until my boots were on the ground and I slammed my truck's door that the man I'd come here for opened his door and stepped onto the rotted and warped boards that made up a dilapidated front porch.

The man looked to be somewhere in his fifties. He was of average height with a stocky build that had my teeth grinding together and my fists clenching so tight my knuckles turned white. His gut spoke to drinking too much booze, but the rest of him was solid, from his shoulders to his legs.

This guy had serious height and weight on Serenity. Too fucking much. If he'd wanted to, he could have done some serious damage to a small thing like her. I suddenly had the desire to wring her smooth, delicate neck for putting herself in such a dangerous situation.

"This is private land. You've got no right bein' here."

I was sure the man was packing. If it wasn't on his person, odds were, it was right inside the door, at easy reach. Knowing that didn't stop me, but I kept my steps measured and calm.

"This'll only take a minute, then we'll be on our way. We just have a message to deliver."

Bryce stayed at the base of the steps as I climbed them —careful to keep the hitch in my step from the prosthesis from showing—to face off with the man.

He crossed his arms over his barrel chest as he eyed me up and down. I didn't miss the way his throat worked on a thick swallow. He might have been big enough to do some damage to Serenity, but I was a whole different story. I could crush this fucker like a bug.

"Don't see how you got anything to say I wanna hear."

I stopped with only about a foot between us and spoke through gritted teeth. "Oh, you'll want to hear this. And you'll want to take my words to heart. Believe me."

The man's eyes narrowed, nothing but dark, fathomless hatred in their dull depths. This was a man who woke up mad at the world every morning and went to bed every night blaming it for his shortcomings. He was a miserable fuck who would never be happy with anything.

He jerked his chin up in a failed attempt to intimidate. "Think it'd be smart to get the fuck off my land. Or we'll move you off ourselves."

My lips pulled up, the humorless smirk on my face more intimidating than his pathetic chin jerk, and I knew that by the way the color slowly leached from his ruddy cheeks. "Close confines like this, I can promise you won't get to that gun you got stashed behind the door before my knife's out of the sheath tucked at my back and the blade's pressed against your throat. But if you want to try it, be my guest."

He blinked.

"And before you think any of your piece-of-shit hill-billy brothers can save you, my boy back there's a much faster draw and a hell of a better shot. Pretty sure you're smart enough to know who we are, so you also know I'm not lying."

Cyrus cast his eyes to something or someone over my shoulder, giving the person an almost imperceptible shake of the head.

"Smart choice. I got word you were in my town today, causing a scene and stirring up trouble."

"What I do with my boy ain't got nothin' to do with you. I suggest you mind your own business."

"See, that's where you're wrong. Your boy lives in my town, that means he's got us looking out for him. As far as you're concerned, that kid's no longer on your radar, and Hope Valley's nothing more than a memory. I catch wind you've set foot in my town or even so much as breathed that foul, sour-rot breath of yours in that boy's direction, I'm going to come back here, and my next visit won't be near as civilized."

His arrogance and narcissism wouldn't allow him to back down or cower, even though he knew he didn't stand a chance. His Adam's apple bobbed in a telltale show of fear. "You threatening me?"

"Goddamn right I am. And you don't want me to have to come out and do it again." I took a single step back.

"Now, nod your head to tell me you understand what I'm saying so I can get the fuck out of this hellhole."

His jaw worked back and forth, and I could actually hear his teeth grind. We continued to stare at one another. I kept my eyes pinned to his but caught the way his fists clenched and flexed at his sides.

Unlike him, I was a patient man. I could out-wait him. However, it didn't take long for him to give in, and he finally nodded.

I didn't bother hanging around for another second. I simply turned my back on the asshole and walked back to my truck. He wasn't worth turning back for.

Fourteen

Serenity

"I'm on my way, I swear. I just need to change really fast and touch up my hair and makeup."

I flew into my apartment like a tornado, whipping my shirt over my head and tossing it aside somewhere in the living room. My boots were kicked off on the move, and my jeans were discarded somewhere in the hallway.

"Jesus, Sere," Stella said in my ear. "Are you okay? It sounds like a stampede is moving through your apartment."

I managed to balance my cellphone between my ear and shoulder as I slipped and slid on my socks the rest of the way to my bedroom before colliding with my closet door. "I'm fine. Just trying to hurry so I'm not even later. It took me longer to get out of the bar than it should have, but I had a table of frat assholes who thought their shit didn't stink and it would be funny to mess with their waitress."

It meant losing out on a whole table's worth of tips when Rory had them ousted, but honestly, it was worth it. They were drunk enough to think the word "no" was a challenge, and if they hadn't been removed, I would have ended up kicking at least one of them in the balls so hard they'd never be able to have kids. Not that the world wouldn't be a better place if they weren't able to procreate.

"Will you relax," my sister said through the line. "I told you, you don't need to rush. We're happy to wait for you."

I spoke as I flicked through the hangers in my closet, trying to find the perfect outfit. "I know, I'm just excited. I haven't had a girls' night out in—" I paused to try and remember back, only to come to a startling conclusion. "Damn, I guess I've *never* had a girls' night. Not that hanging with you and Kira doesn't count." But it was a sad reality that the closest I'd had to a girlfriend in too many years to count was my sister-in-law.

Stella's voice was soft and gentle as it came through the line. "I know what you mean. I didn't really notice my lack of a social life until I moved here either. I love our family, and we always have fun together, but there's something to be said for having a crew that isn't related to you in one way or another."

"You get it," I said with a grin as I came to a stop at a little black dress that would be *perfect* for tonight. "All right, I'm hanging up so I can finish getting ready."

"Okay, sis. See you soon."

I disconnected and tossed the phone onto my bed

before fishing through my dresser drawer for my strapless bra I needed in order to wear the dress I'd picked out.

Since moving to Hope Valley two months ago, I'd grown accustomed to living the jeans and T-shirt kind of life. There was something to be said for living life comfortably, especially when, in my past life, I'd had to dress myself up to the nines in order to attract whatever man was my target for the evening.

I was more than happy to leave that all behind, but sometimes a woman just wanted to dress up and hit the town with her girls, and that was exactly what I had planned for the night.

There was a club one town over called Whiskey Dolls that was one of the best burlesque clubs in all of Virginia and the surrounding states. I'd heard all about it and had desperately wanted to go, but I'd never really had the time to waste, standing in a line that wrapped around the whole damn building. Fortunately, a few of the women we were going with tonight were friends with the owners and a few of the Whiskey Dolls themselves, so not only were we getting through the door without waiting, we also had a table reserved just for us.

I couldn't remember the last time I was this excited to hit a club.

I was a pro at making quick work of my hair and makeup and was out the door fifteen minutes later.

The air had a bit of a chill to it as I climbed out of my car in the back of the parking lot and started toward the entrance, making the pine scent in the air even crisper. As I bundled myself tighter inside my coat and picked up the pace, I couldn't wait to see what Hope Valley looked like in the winter. The town was beautiful in the summer and fall, especially with the leaves changing colors, making the surrounding mountains look like a sea of fire, but I bet once the valley was covered in fresh white powder, it would look like a snow globe.

I heard my sister's excited voice as soon as I rounded the corner. "There she is!"

I opened my arms so Stella could walk right into them. My sister and I had always been close, hell, she was my best friend, but our relationship had changed recently.

We hadn't grown apart. Just the opposite, in fact. But the difference came with the fact that she was blissfully, unapologetically happy. All her life she'd hated what we'd done. She'd kept it to herself, letting it eat at her until it nearly made her sick, but she'd always wished for a different life.

She'd been lonely, feeling like the odd man out in our family of grifters. Because she hadn't been honest with us, she didn't know that Spencer and I hadn't been too thrilled with our lot in life either. She thought she was the black sheep. But once the truth finally came out, that we all wanted better lives for ourselves, somehow a relationship that was already strong became titanium. Nothing could ever break it.

Then there was the matter of us being kidnapped together. There was just something about kicking the ass of the man who'd abducted us that solidified the bonds of sisterhood.

Now she was happier than she'd ever been, living her dream life with her dream man, and I . . . well, minus the man part, I didn't have many complaints about my new life. I loved working at the Tap Room. I even liked my tiny apartment, mainly because I paid for it honestly with hard work.

"I'm so glad you were able to come tonight," she said once we broke apart. "This is going to be so much fun."

"I'm glad too."

"Oh my God," a voice behind me spoke, and I turned just as Sage reached my side, her gaze cast downward. "You got them. And they look *hot*."

I glanced down at my stiletto-clad feet, lifting the left one to flex and twirl, showing off the shoes we'd talked about only a couple weeks back. "I sure did. And this is the first chance I've had to wear them. I'm glad I finally had an excuse."

My sister did a quick round of introductions. There were a few familiar faces in the crowd, such as Sage, Eden, and Gypsy. Then there was a stunning redhead named Nona, and two close friends of Sage's: Danika, who owned Muffin Top, the best freaking coffee house in the US of A, and Hayden.

A second later, the bouncer, a huge wall of burly, intimidating man, stepped aside and held the door open for us without even checking the clipboard in his hand, and we were heading inside.

A woman dressed in a vintage cigarette girl uniform met us in the entryway and led us to our table. It was barely nine o'clock, but the place was already packed to capacity.

"Wow," I breathed, as we slipped into the massive red velvet U-shaped booth in the very center of the floor. "This place is incredible."

It was obvious this was the best table in the whole place. From our vantage point, we had a perfect, unobstructed view of the stage. It was currently empty and dark, but that was only because the show hadn't started yet.

Gypsy looked at me with a waggle of her brows. "Doll, you haven't seen anything yet."

———

The song blasting through the speakers ended, the bright spotlights lighting the stage shut off, and the entire club erupted.

After a couple drinks and some mouthwatering appetizers while being engulfed in a seriously cool as hell ambiance, I was starting to think I understood what all the hype was about.

But then a few of the Whiskey Dolls hit the stage for a performance, and I realized the club could get even better.

I'd cheered and whistled for the women who just finished their number so loudly my throat was starting to feel scratchy.

"Oh my God," I exclaimed over the raucous applause, leaning into our table so my crew could hear me. "They were *incredible*! I've never seen anything like that. This place is the *tits*."

Sage shuffled closer to me in the booth so she could be heard easier. "The one that was on the far left, that's our girl, Charlotte. She's married to Dalton. He's another Alpha Omega dude. She's cool as hell. You'll really like her when you get a chance to meet her."

I had no doubt about that. So far, I'd really come to like everyone I'd met since moving to town. Well, with the exception of Sue Ellen Mayfield, but from what I'd been able to gather, I was in the majority with that one.

"She'll be at our next girls' night in," Eden said. "Once a month, we all shift our schedules around so we can meet up at someone's house to gossip and drink and give each other facials." Her doe-eyes went even wider, like she'd just had the most brilliant idea. "You should totally come! It's so much fun. You'll fit right in."

It sounded like it, and I had to admit, I loved hearing that I'd fit in. Growing up a Ryan, I'd never had the luxury of having sleepovers with my girlfriends. I'd seen countless movies where the popular girl had all her friends over. They'd do each other's hair and give each other makeovers, and I'd desperately wanted something like that.

Sitting in the booth, surrounded by all these awesome women, I felt that little hole inside me, the one teenaged-Serenity never had the chance to fill, growing smaller and smaller.

"You had me at gossip and drink. The facials are just an added bonus."

Eden beamed at me, like I'd made her day instead of it being the other way around. "Great. I'll text you with the details."

I couldn't wait.

Hayden, a stunning woman with beautiful strawberry blonde hair spoke next. "So how do you like Hope Valley so far?"

Like Stella and me, she's been a transplant from the city. She'd moved here to take over her aunt's flower shop after finding out her husband at the time had been banging her best friend. She divorced his loser ass, settled in a new town, and met a new man, one who was hotter than her ex and treated her like she was the most precious thing he'd ever owned.

I loved hearing her story; in fact, all these women had stories that kept me on the edge of my seat all night.

"I love it," I answered. "I'll be honest, I wasn't sure about going from the city to a smaller town. I worried I'd get bored, but things here aren't as quiet as I'd expected."

Snorts and laughter filled our table. Between the women around me there had been more abductions, stalkers, and showdowns with bad guys than I ever thought possible. Seemed like, just when things started to level out in Hope Valley, something came in and stirred the dust back up. So far, everything that had gone down had a happy ending, so that was something.

"Yeah, it's a sweet town and a great place to live," Nona

started, "but it's certainly not boring. Even if no one's being kidnapped, you still have people like Mrs. McClintock going around, talking about breaking her new hips in."

I hadn't had the luxury of meeting the eighty-something blue-haired woman she was talking about, but I'd heard rumors, and I was looking forward to the day I crossed paths with the blunt-as-hell, cantankerous old woman.

"I hear you already experienced your first showdown at the bar not too long ago," Gypsy said, reminding me of what had happened with Fletcher's biological father.

A shiver worked its way down my spine as I thought back to that man's hate-filled eyes. Evil eyes. That was the only way I could think to describe him.

I lifted my martini glass, swallowing back a healthy sip to try and dull the effects of that memory. "Yeah, it wasn't pleasant. I just hope he got the message and leaves Fletcher alone. I'm worried that just as he's getting his feet on solid ground, the shithead will pop back up and ruin everything he's worked so hard for. He's such a good kid. He deserves better."

Stella reached out and placed her hand in mine, giving it a reassuring squeeze. "If he's got you in his corner, I have no doubt he'll be okay."

Man, but I had the best sister in the freaking world.

FIFTEEN
SERENITY

"Enough about the dark stuff," Sage harrumphed, lifting her cocktail in the air. "What I want to know is what's happening between Serenity and the last bachelor standing!"

I choked on the sip of martini I just took, the vodka burning my nose and throat, making my eyes water violently.

For some reason, that sent the table into hysterics. Even Stella was giggling wildly as she patted my back and lifted one of my arms to help me out.

"What?" I croaked once I'm able to breathe, lifting the cloth napkin from my lap to carefully dab at the tears that had brimmed in my eyes. The last thing I needed was to screw up my mascara.

I was quickly coming to find that Sage was the kind of woman who said whatever was on her mind. Usually, that was something I'd love, seeing as I was similar in that way. But in this instant, not so much.

I felt heat creep up my neck and center in my cheeks, making them burn bright red. Clearing my throat, I put the martini glass down and moved to the glass of water beside it, sucking some of the cool icy liquid down my burning throat. I could feel Stella's gaze on me the whole time, and sure enough, when I looked over, her head was tilted to the side, her shrewd gaze full of curiosity.

"I don't know what you're talking about. There's nothing going on between us."

I felt the lasered focus of everyone at our table. I knew it was only my imagination, but it was like a hush had fallen over the entire bar, and I was the center of *everyone's* attention.

Sage pinched her lips to the side, her expression screaming, *oh please. Who do you think you're fooling*? She lifted her cocktail glass and swirled the amber liquid inside before taking a sip. "Really? Because that's not what I heard."

"Oh my God," Nona gasped as she practically threw herself across to table to better see Sage. "What did you hear?"

"She didn't hear anything!" I insisted. "Because there's nothing to hear."

The whole table chose to ignore me, and I was suddenly questioning why I thought it was such a brilliant idea to make friends in the first damn place.

"Well, I heard from Rory that Hunter found out from Cord what was going down at the bar, and that, even though it was being handled, Hunter stormed out of the office like the hounds of hell were nipping at his heels and practically got into a wreck on his way to the bar."

I switched back to my martini and drank deeply. I was going to kill Rory, then I was going after her gossipy-ass husband. Damn me for deciding to drive instead of calling for an Uber, because I *really* needed another drink. "I'm sure that's an exaggeration."

Sage shrugged casually. "Maybe, maybe not. But she said he blew into the bar and made a beeline straight to our girl. Didn't even spare anyone else a glance."

My stomach began doing Olympic-gymnast level flips.

Don't read into it, Serenity, I silently scolded, knowing this was a road I certainly didn't need to go down.

She waggled her eyebrows suggestively as she added, "Then he dragged her into the back, and they were locked in the office, all alone, for several minutes."

I waved my hands and tried talking over the chorus of oohs and aahs. "No, no, no. It wasn't like that. He only did that so he could yell at me in private for putting myself in a dangerous situation."

Stella's eyebrows shot up. "And you let him walk out of there alive?" she asked in complete bewilderment. She knew me too well. If it had been any other man, he'd have spent the next week walking around with an icepack down his shorts.

Even Spencer hadn't been immune to my wrath when we were growing up. He took his role as overprotective big brother very seriously and took it upon himself to threaten any guy who showed even the slightest bit of interest in me.

When I finally found one who was willing to risk a beatdown from my brother, he informed him I wasn't allowed to go on the date the boy had asked me on. I gave him a chance to take it back. It wasn't my fault he didn't heed my warning. It also wasn't my fault that he had to get his nose reset after I drove my fist into it. After all, he was the one who taught me to punch.

I bit down on my bottom lip under the scrutiny of the women sitting around the table. "I would have, if he didn't have a point," I admitted. "I kind of lost my shit when I saw how scared Fletcher was, and I acted without thinking."

Stella nodded in agreement. "That's on par with your personality."

I shot her a murderous look. "Anyway. That's all it was. There's nothing happening between Hunter and me."

"Rory also said he's been coming into the bar a lot more than he used to."

I shifted my scowl from my sister to Sage. "Rory would do well to keep her mouth shut."

The table burst into laughter.

However, she wasn't totally off the mark. She wasn't

the only one who'd noticed that Hunter's visits to the Tap Room had picked up. Not only did he come in for a cold beer or two after work nearly every night I was working, but he'd taken to coming in for lunch on the days I had the early shift. He usually sat in my section, but if not, he was on a barstool at the end of the bar where the servers lined up to put in their orders, always ready for a conversation. I wasn't sure if he knew my schedule, or if it was just the world's biggest coincidence, but lately I was seeing more of Hunter McCann than anyone else. And those damn shivers and belly flips *still* hadn't gone away.

"We're just friends. That's all."

God, when would it stop stinging to say that?

In my defense, it wasn't like he was making it easy. His words and his actions were a constant contradiction, and it was starting to do my head in. Just when I'd get myself to a place where I'd think the whole friendship thing would work, he did something like bringing me lunch from Evergreen Diner because I'd mentioned craving Ralph's meatball sub. Or he'd walk me to my car after a shift and linger once I was safely at my car long enough to brush a strand of hair behind my ear.

If there was a chance for him to touch me, he never failed to take it. And my skin never failed to erupt with goosebumps at the feel of his rough hands on my skin.

The shadows still lurked deep in his eyes, but they didn't look nearly as dark as they had when I'd first met him. I kept telling myself that it wasn't because of me, but that stupid niggling ember of hope deep down inside me refused to be snuffed out, and every time he did something to make me think he could possibly want something more than friendship, that ember would glow brighter and hotter, like a coal being doused in lighter fluid.

Sage didn't look convinced. She shook her head while nibbling on her bottom lip. "I don't know. He's seemed different the past couple of weeks."

I tried my hardest not to let her words fuel that stupid coal, but then my sister spoke up. "She's right. I mean, I don't know him super well, but it's like he's been in a better mood lately."

Sage nodded. "He's been especially grumpy the past few months. It's been nice to see him getting back to normal."

I wasn't exactly sure what normal was for Hunter, but I would have been lying if I said that wasn't nice to hear. It also piqued my curiosity, and I couldn't help but wonder what had happened a few months back to put him in the mood he'd been in since I'd known him.

My mind spun in a thousand different directions as our server returned to our table with a tray of refills.

I felt the tingle of eyes on me and turned to find my sister looking straight at me, her brow marred by an all-too-familiar wrinkle of concern. It was a look she wore damn near constantly in my old life. She worried about me. It should have been the other way around, given that I was the older sister, but Stella had always been a bit of a nurturer.

And it didn't help that she could read me like a book.

She knew I couldn't leave a puzzle unsolved and that my love of a good challenge had gotten me in trouble more times than I could count. She'd already been concerned about my growing fixation with Hunter McCann, as it was. The little nugget that had just dropped in my lap certainly wasn't going to help put her mind at ease.

Unbeknownst to the rest of the women around us, Stella and I had a full-blown conversation, using only our eyes.

She lowered her chin and narrowed her eyes. *I know what you're thinking.*

I widened mine and gave an infinitesimal shake of my head. *I don't know what you're talking about.*

Her glare was so tiny, it didn't register to anyone but me. *Bullshit. I know you. This is a real-life human being, Sere, not a puzzle for ages six and up. You can't fix him or solve him.*

My chest rose and fell on a huff. *Who said that's what I want to do?*

Damn her for knowing me so well. Because that was *exactly* what I wanted to do.

Her brows drooped and her head canted to the side. *I just don't want to see you get hurt.*

God, I loved my sister. That could probably go without saying, but I couldn't help it. She was, hands down, the best person I knew.

I smiled and leaned in to bump her shoulder with mine. *I love you too, little sis. Don't worry about me.*

I knew the conversation was over when she let out a sigh and lifted her drink to her lips for a deep pull.

I lifted my own and sipped, determined to push thoughts of Hunter McCann from my mind for the rest of the evening.

SIXTEEN
SERENITY

As much as I loved my new heels, and I *seriously* loved them, I was ready to kick them off and store them in my closet for at least three months. I hoped the feeling in my toes would return. As beautiful as they were, they were like torture devices when worn for more than a couple hours.

As soon as I was parked in front of my apartment building, I threw my door open and twisted in my seat so I could bend forward and slide my feet free of their prison. With heels in hand, I started up the sidewalk, barefooted.

The night had been more fun than I'd expected. Not only did we get to watch the Whiskey Dolls perform, but Gypsy also pulled strings so we could go backstage and meet the dancers. For being somewhat of local celebrities, the girls were all cool as hell. Sage had been right, I liked Charlotte instantly. Hell, I liked all of them, including the owner, a beautiful, bubbly, talented woman by the name of McKenna.

By the time we called it a night, my phone had been full of brand-new numbers, and I had several plans to meet up for coffee or drinks or dinner.

It was in that thought that I shoved my key into the deadbolt to unlock my door, only for it to swing open before I could react. A hand lashed out, grabbing a fistful of my hair and using it to yank me through the door.

Pain lanced through my scalp, making me cry out as the door was thrown shut and I was slammed back into it so hard my head thumped violently against the solid wood.

I opened my mouth to scream when the figure placed a hand at my throat and began to squeeze, cutting the sound off, along with my air.

Panic shredded my insides to ribbons as I struggled and clawed at the hand squeezing my throat in a bruising grip, but the thick work gloves prevented me from breaking skin. I kicked and thrashed, trying to break free, but it was no use.

The person holding me captive leaned in closer, and for the first time, I paused long enough to take him in. The apartment was pitch black, with the curtains drawn and the lights off, but he brought his face close enough for me to make his features out in the darkness, and when I did, icy fear reached into my chest and clutched my heart.

"This is what happens to little whores who don't mind their own business."

The rank smell of cigarettes came off his breath as he hissed in my face, making my stomach roil.

"Please," I wheezed, my voice a panful rasp.

"That's right, bitch. Let me hear you beg. Told you someone would teach you a lesson, didn't I?"

I couldn't remember a time when I'd been more scared. Even the asshole who'd kidnapped Stella and me hadn't elicited this kind of fear. But that was because it had only taken a matter of seconds to realize he was a brainless shithead.

This man, on the other hand, was a different story. He'd scared me from our first encounter.

Icy hands gripped my insides, but I refused to let them freeze me in place. I was a wildcat, damn it. I fought. And I wasn't going to let this asshole make me cower or beg.

Since clawing at his hand at my throat wasn't doing anything, I decided to change tactics and went for his face, digging my nails into his cheeks as deep as I could get them.

He reared back on a pained holler but didn't release his grip on my throat.

My ears started to ring and the edges of my vision began to grow dark. If I didn't break his hold soon, I was going to pass out . . . or worse.

I curled my lips back, baring my teeth, and shoved my thumbs into his eye sockets. He reared back on a shout, but his grip finally loosened. I wanted to keel over, brace my hands on my knees and suck in all the air I'd so desperately been lacking a moment ago, but there wasn't time. As he stumbled back, I spun around, scrambling for the door-knob. I felt the gust of wind that came with his hand waving past, trying to grab hold of me.

But I was already running, screaming as loud as my bruised, gravelly voice would allow.

———

I had the headache to end all headaches, and the flashing blue and white lights filling the parking lot weren't help-ing. Neither was that stupid penlight the paramedic was currently shining in my eyes as she instructed me to follow it.

It wasn't her fault, she was only doing her job, but that light was having the same effect as nails on a chalkboard.

I was exhausted, experiencing an adrenaline crash stronger than I'd experienced before, but something told me my night wasn't close to being over. Especially since Cyrus Whitlock had taken off while I was inside my neigh-bor's apartment, calling 911.

He was in the wind, as they say.

I knew I was right when I heard my sister's voice through the din of noise all around me. "Where is she? Where's my sister? Serenity—" she started to shout, then made her way through the sea of police cars and spotted me from the back of the ambulance I was currently sitting in, being checked over. West stopped at her back, his expression looking downright murderous.

"Oh my God." Her hands came up to cover her mouth and tears instantly filled her eyes.

"I'm okay," I said, only I sounded like someone had taken sandpaper to my vocal cords, and if I were being honest, it kind of felt that way too. Who knew being choked could cause so much lasting pain?

I lowered the icepack I'd been holding against the knot on the back of my head and attempted to stand, only to have the paramedic *and* Stella rush to prevent me from moving.

"Just stay sitting," Stella ordered, her features growing fierce despite the tears leaving tracks down her face. Like me, she was still in the cute, trendy dress she'd worn at the club, only, where I was barefooted, having lost my gorgeous stilettos in the chaos of the past half hour, she was still wearing her heels.

A breeze blew in just then, sending a shiver skating down my back. Before I could nestle deeper into the itchy blanket the paramedic had draped over my shoulders, Stella pulled it tighter and began rubbing up and down my arms in an attempt to warm me up. Whether it was the temperature outside or everything that had happened, I wasn't sure if it was possible for me to feel warm.

"What the hell happened?" Stella finally asked.

"Took the question right out of my mouth." My sister and I both turned at the same time as two men sauntered up to my ambulance. At their presence, the paramedic took off.

The one who had just spoken gave me a kind smile.

"Ms. Ryan. I'm detective Leo Drake, and this is my partner, Micah Langford. We understand you've had a hell of a night. We have a few questions, but we promise we'll try to make this as quick as possible."

So these were the men who put rings on Danika's and Hayden's fingers. Good for them, because *dayum*.

"Call me Serenity," I rasped. "After all, your wives have become two of my favorite people."

My initial reaction was to get my hackles up. To make some sort of excuse and bail before the police could do any digging into me. But then I remembered I wasn't the one in trouble. These detectives were here to help *me*. Because I hadn't done anything wrong. *I* was the one who was attacked and assaulted. They were here because they were going to catch the asshole who'd done it.

I started to recall what happened as soon as I got home, but given how much it hurt to speak, it was taking twice as long. As I told the officers everything, the crowd around us had steadily grown. Most of the women I'd spent the better part of the evening with had shown up, their men in tow. Somehow, Rory had gotten word about what happened, and she and Cord came flying into the parking lot only about a minute or two after my own parents had shown up.

With a small child and a pregnant wife at home, Spencer hadn't been able to pick up and make the middle of the night drive to me, but he was currently on FaceTime with my father, getting the whole scoop, and cussing a blue streak.

With each ticking second, more and more of those ridiculously hot Alpha Omega guys had arrived on the scene, each of them looking pissed as hell as their wives coddled me the best they could.

But it wasn't until I'd nearly finished recounting the night that the atmosphere suddenly grew charged, the air all around crackling menacingly. I didn't have to look to see what had caused the change.

A break formed in the crowd of people around me, and Hunter suddenly appeared. As if reading the situation, everyone either scattered like roaches after a light had been turned on, or they hung back, close enough to watch the drama play out from the safety of the sidelines.

Well, everyone except my family, that was. And the two detectives, of course.

His blue eyes were so cold, I worried I might get frostbite from a single look. The biting, chilling rage radiating off him had me cocooning even deeper into the blanket in the hopes of disappearing.

"Who?" One word had never been so shiver-inducing.

Lincoln stepped in, apparently not afraid to wade into whatever was about to unfold here. "Hunter, man, why don't we go talk over here—?"

I couldn't say the same for myself. As drawn to him as I was, and as much as I usually wanted to be around him, I had to admit that Hunter was kind of scaring me just then.

"Not moving from this fucking spot until I get a goddamn name."

"I get it man," Leo started. "You want to make this guy

pay. We all do. But you need to stay cool. We can't have you doing something that'll screw with our investigation."

Hunter slowly turned his head and regarded Leo in a way that would have had me peeing my pants in fear. I had to hand it to the other man, he withstood the scrutiny surprisingly well.

"Wait. What's going on?" My brother's inanimate voice rang out into the night from my father's phone. "Who's talking? Is that that huge behemoth of a dude Serenity was playing pool with at Stella's engagement party?"

For the love of all that was holy. Leave it to my big brother to make a tense situation awkward as hell. It was like a gift or something.

Stella leaned into my dad and lifted up on her tiptoes to see the screen better. Her voice was somewhat hushed, but not enough that every single person in the area couldn't hear what she was saying.

"His name is Hunter McCann, and yes."

"Someone give him that fucker's name," Spencer called out. "He'll take care of that shit, and I'm willing to bet no one would ever find the body."

I couldn't keep my mouth shut for another second. "Shut up, Spence! You aren't helping."

That had been a mistake. At the sound of my messed-up voice, Hunter went from pissed to fire-breathing. He closed the rest of the distance between us, ignoring everyone around like they didn't even exist.

I flinched when he reached out for me, causing the

hand traveling in my direction to stop, midair. His jaw muscles ticked, the cord in his neck strained. "You don't ever have to be scared of me, Wildcat," he husked in that deep timbre of his that always made me melt. "Not *ever*."

"Sorry," I croaked. "It's just been a long night. It's not as bad as it looks, believe me."

If only I didn't sound like I'd suddenly taken up smoking three packs a day.

"It was him, wasn't it?"

I didn't have to ask what *him* Hunter was talking about. With a resigned sigh, I nodded my head, because I knew refusing to answer would only prolong the inevitable. I had a gut feeling Hunter was the type of man used to getting what he wanted. So if he wanted to know who hurt me, it was only a matter of time.

His hand resumed its earlier journey, gently grabbing hold of the blanket and pulling it aside, giving me nothing to hide the damage that had been done to my neck beneath.

The instant the bruises were revealed, Hunter let out a hiss between his teeth, my mother burst into tears, and Stella let out an uncharacteristic string of curse words that was more fitting for Spencer.

"That's it," my dad declared, his fist white-knuckling around his phone so tight I worried he'd shatter the damn thing. "I'll pack you a bag. You're coming home with me and your mom."

A whole new type of panic set in then, making my back shoot straight and my eyes go wide. I shot a horrified look in Stella's direction, silently praying she'd help me get out of this somehow.

"Uh, Dad, you know what? That's not necessary. She can come stay with me and West. We live closer."

My shoulders slumped on a relieved breath. It wasn't that I didn't like spending time with my parents. I absolutely did. In small doses.

With everything that had just gone down, my father would have spent the next few days pacing and raging every time he looked at me and saw the bruises before taking to the front porch with a shotgun like we lived in the Wild West or something. Then my mom would have cried and fussed and helicoptered until I went crazy.

It was best for everyone involved if I let them coddle in short spurts.

I opened my mouth, ready to agree quickly so we could all move on, when Hunter spoke up, directing his penetrating gaze to the paramedic who'd been working on me earlier. "What's the verdict? Does she need to go to the hospital?"

The woman looked back at me, her expression thoughtful as she scrutinized me. "Well, it doesn't look like she has a concussion, just a nasty knot. The real problem is her throat. It's going to be hurting her for a while. There isn't much the hospital can do for that besides pain management."

"And I don't need that," I insisted. "I feel fine. Nothing a couple Tylenol won't fix. I'll be good as new before you know it."

He nodded resolutely, coming to a decision in his head I hadn't been privy to. He turned on the group, giving me his back. "Gypsy, Stella, Eden. Go pack her a bag with enough stuff to last her at least a week."

"What—"

He kept talking. "Linc. Do me a favor and take her back to my place."

My chin jerked back in bewilderment, the movement sending a stab of pain through my neck. "Wait. What? Why? Stella said—"

Hunter whipped around on me, skewering me with a look that said it was best not to argue. "This isn't up for debate. You're staying with me for the foreseeable future."

My mouth dropped open. I looked around the group, but everyone seemed resigned to take orders. Hell, even Stella nodded her head.

My mom came over and placed a kiss on my temple before hugging me from the side. "It's for the best, sweetie. You'll be safe with him, I'm sure."

She didn't even know Hunter! How could she possibly know that?

"But—"

"Stay with her until I get back," Hunter said to Lincoln. "Got some shit I need to take care of."

"Hunter," Micah said, his tone admonishing, "don't go off and start shit we won't be able to cover, damn it."

"Fucking hell." Lincoln raked a hand through his blond hair. The man looked like he belonged on a Viking ship, not corralling a bunch of former military commando types. He jabbed his finger at Hunter, semi-repeating, "You heard them. Don't make this harder, you got me?"

Hunter simply nodded before spinning on the heel of his motorcycle boot and disappearing the way he came.

"Marco," Lincoln clipped, jolting my attention back to him.

"Yeah, boss."

"Follow him. Make sure he doesn't do anything that'll get him arrested.

"On it."

Marco disappeared as well, and I was left with one question only.

"What the hell just happened?"

SEVENTEEN

SERENITY

I felt like I was moving on autopilot, my brain covered in a layer of fuzz my conscious mind couldn't penetrate. My whole body felt heavy, my limbs weighed down with exhaustion. I was so damn tired by the time Lincoln pulled up to Hunter's house that I could barely keep my eyes open.

After packing my largest suitcase so full I hadn't been able to lift the damn thing to put it in the back of Lincoln's truck, my sister had insisted on coming with us to, in her words, get me settled.

Truthfully, I was glad to have her with me, the one known in a sea of unknown I was currently experiencing. First, I was being chauffeured around by a man I barely knew. Sure, he seemed nice, and had been extremely careful with me, but the most I knew of him was that his name was Lincoln, he was my sister's boss, and was married to one of my new friends, Eden. Second was the fact I was being shipped off to a place I'd never been in my life.

I was so tired by the time we pulled onto the short tree-lined lane that led to Hunter's house, that I didn't even have the energy to scope out my surroundings.

Lincoln hefted my suitcase out of the bed of his truck and rolled it behind him as he led us up a walkway that was shrouded in shadows from the surrounding trees and let us into a dark house by using a code on the keypad lock instead of an actual key.

"Go ahead and make yourself comfortable, sweetheart," he said after flipping on the lights and holding the door open. "I'm going to make a quick phone call and be right back."

The door snicked shut behind him, leaving Stella and me alone for the first time all night.

"Well," she breathed as she looked around. "At least it's clean, right? That's a pleasant surprise."

I didn't have the energy to do anything more than grunt out in agreement.

A look of sympathy washed over her face before she reached out and took my arm. "Come on, big sis. We'll get you settled and then you can take a shower and crawl into a nice, warm bed. How's that sound?"

It sounded like heaven, honestly. Unfortunately, when we moved down the hallway in search of a guest room, we found that a nice, warm bed wasn't in the cards for me.

The first spare room held a desk and set of shelves, clearly designed to be a home office, and the last of the three bedrooms was full of unpacked boxes and extra-large storage containers. It was obviously the room Hunter shoved shit into that he either didn't want to deal with or didn't know what to do with.

Neither room had a bed.

Fortunately, the couch in the living room was over-sized and looked comfy. Also, I was dead on my feet, so I could have happily slept anywhere.

We located the bathroom, and Stella ushered me inside. "You go ahead and get in the shower. I'll bring you your toiletries and get the couch set up for you when you get out."

I leaned my head against her shoulder, pulling in a deep breath. "Have I mentioned lately that you're the best sister a girl could ever hope for?"

"Not in the past few days," she teased.

"Well, you are. And I don't know what I'd ever do without you."

Her arm came around my waist, giving me an affectionate squeeze. "Fortunately for you, you'll never have to find out. She slapped me on my butt with a playful, "Now, git."

I moved into the bathroom, noticing that the white subway tiles were sparkling clean beneath the lights. That was a relief.

I stopped in front of the pedestal sink, bracing my

hands on the rim, and looked up at my reflection in the mirror. My hair looked like a nest of rats was living inside of it, the dark blonde strands no longer artfully curled, but a tangled, scraggly mess. The makeup I'd taken the time to apply perfectly was now smeared, the mascara and eyeliner running down my cheeks and making me look like an extra for *The Walking Dead*.

Deep purple and blue bruises stippled across my throat, the shape of that asshole's fingers clear as day on my skin.

I'd been so looking forward to my first night out with friends in my new town. It had been better than I could have hoped for, and that asshole had to go and ruin it, putting a dark cloud over what had been an incredible night. And the capper on it all, he'd made me lose my favorite shoes!

Unable to stare at my bedraggled reflection for another moment, I turned away from the mirror and stripped out of the dress I'd carefully selected for the night.

I made the water as hot as I could possibly stand it before climbing into the shower and closing the curtain. The spray felt decadent as it beat against my aching muscles, doing wonders to loosen the knots that had formed in my shoulders and back over the past couple hours.

I wasn't sure how long I'd stood there when a gentle knock on the door pulled me from my daze.

"Sere?" Stella's voice called from the other side of the

shower curtain. "I have your toiletries here. And I got you a pair of pajamas too. They're on the toilet."

"Thank you," I rasped.

Once she left, I made quick work of washing that son of a bitch off my skin. Usually, I had a whole routine I performed every time I stepped out of the shower that involved exfoliation, skin care, and moisturizing, but I didn't have the energy for that.

I toweled myself dry and slipped into the silky tank top and matching sleep shorts Stella had brought me. Ever the thoughtful sister, she'd also brought a clip so I could twist my damp hair into a bun on the crown of my head and secure it in place.

She thought of everything. It was why she was the best.

Ready to crawl onto something soft and pass the hell out, I pulled open the bathroom door, releasing the cloud of steam that had filled the small space, and padded down the hall to the living room. Stella had managed to find a couple blankets and a pillow somewhere and had made up the couch so that all I had to do was lie down, something I didn't hesitate doing. I wasn't sure a pillow had ever looked more inviting in my entire life.

I realized she'd stolen it off Hunter's bed the moment I laid my head on it and smelled that manly, spicy scent that was all him. I wasn't ashamed to admit I might have—definitely—nuzzled farther into the pillow and inhaled deeply, pulling as much of his smell into my lungs as I could.

"You good?" Stella asked, coming to sit on the edge of

the sofa cushion. She reached up to brush back some of the damp strands of hair that had escaped my clip, and I knew she was focusing on the bruises on my neck when her forehead dipped into a pained frown.

"I'm great, Stell Bell. Thank you so much for taking care of me. But you should call West to come get you. I'm totally safe here," I assured her, desperately wanting to clear the sadness from her eyes.

She hesitated a moment, worrying her bottom lip between her teeth. "You sure you don't want me to stay with you?"

My lips curved up into a smile. "I'm not sure how that would work. The couch is the only other place to sleep, and you never were one for snuggling."

"I snuggle!" she exclaimed in mock affront. "I'm West's little spoon every damn night. I just didn't like snuggling with you when we were little because you put off more heat than a damn radiator."

I let loose a giggle that quickly turned into a yawn.

"Get some sleep, sis. Linc's right outside if you need him. And I'll talk to you tomorrow, okay?"

My eyelids grew heavy as I blinked up at her. "Okay. Love you."

"Love you too."

Less than a minute later, I was out like a light.

———

Hunter

I twisted the wheel of my truck, turning onto the lane that led to that fucker Cyrus's place so goddamn fast gravel and clumps of dirt spit from my rear tires, pinging off the windshield of Marco's SUV as he followed behind me at Lincoln's instruction.

I didn't slow down until I neared that fucker's trailer. Lights started to flick on in the surrounding trailers and RVs at the sound of my engine, and by the time I slammed on the brakes and my truck skidded to a stop, kicking up a plume of dust, doors were flying open.

I threw the door of my truck open and started moving the instant my boots hit the ground.

"Back inside," I heard Marco bark at the other people, but I was too focused on what was in front of me to pay attention to anyone else.

As if sensing my murderous mood, the dog that was still tied to that gnarled tree stopped barking, letting out a scared whine before burrowing under the shoddy front stoop to hide.

My footsteps were like thunder, matching the deep, resonating pitch of my heartbeat, as I stormed up the rickety steps, then, without so much as taking a breath, I lifted my foot and slammed it into the shitty wood, sending it flying open and breaking right off the hinges.

"Whitlock!" I shouted into the darkness.

But his wasn't the response I got. "Jesus Christ,"

Marco hissed as he rushed in after me, gun in hand. I was so determined to get to Cyrus Whitlock, I hadn't taken the time to get my own from the glovebox. Not smart. I knew that. But I wasn't feeling particularly smart at the moment. "What's the fucking plan here, Hunter?"

There was no plan. Clearly.

The only thing that had been going through my head as I drove up here was the image of those bruises on Serenity's smooth, delicate neck. The only thing I could hear was the sound of her damaged voice. And this fucker was the one who'd done that to her.

When she cowered away from me, my wildcat crouching in fear because of what he'd put her through, my vision stained red. I wanted to make him pay for doing that to her.

"Fuck me," Marco continued to grumble as he followed me through the disgusting trailer home, gun aimed and at the ready in case anything were to pop out at us. "You can't just kick someone's door open and let yourself in."

"Just fucking did," I gritted through clenched teeth.

I charged through the house with all the grace of a raging bull, but other than the trash the asshole left behind —and there was a lot of it—the pitiful excuse for a house was empty. The place wasn't even fit for rats, let alone a human being. I wasn't sure whether or not the place had been any better when Fletcher lived here, but I wouldn't have been surprised if that boy had been tasked with keeping things clean, and his prick of a father let it go to hell once he was alone.

I stopped in the middle of the living room, scanning the space. There was a beat-up recliner with a sunken cushion that indicated where Cyrus Whitlock spent most of his time, and a threadbare couch that leaned to the left due to a broken leg. Beer cans and takeout bags lay crumpled on the stained carpet.

"He's not here anyway." I clenched my fists so tight my blunt nails cut into the skin of my palms. I couldn't remember the last time I'd wanted to beat the living hell out of another human being so badly.

I was craving the bite of pain in my knuckles that would have come with breaking every bone in his face.

"Of course he's not," Marco clipped, finally lowering his piece now that it was clear there was no immediate threat. "You think he'd actually be stupid enough to come back here after the shit he pulled tonight? Of course not. Leo and Micah sent units to the surrounding hospitals and clinics. Apparently, Serenity did some damage herself."

I turned to look at him over my shoulder, lifting a brow in silent question.

He shook his head and raked his fingers through his hair. "When clawing the shit out of his face didn't break his hold, she jabbed her thumbs into his eye sockets to get him to let go. That's how she got away from him."

My fucking wildcat.

"With any luck, he'll turn up somewhere, looking to

get patched up." He blew out a huff. "If there's a God, the asshole would be blinded for life."

One could hope but given the fact he was able to get away, I doubted it.

I didn't know what the hell to do with the rage that was eating at my insides, but I knew I couldn't stay here all night, hoping he'd crawl out from beneath whatever rock he was hiding under.

We started out of the trailer, stepping over the door I'd busted to hell, just as one of the neighbors stepped up onto the porch.

"This is private property! You've got no right—"

Marco drew his gun at the sight of the rifle the hillbilly had in his hands, but before anyone could come close to pulling a trigger, I snatched the weasely guy up by his throat and slammed him back against the side of the trailer.

With my free hand, I yanked the rifle from his flimsy hold and passed it to Marco. "That's the last time you come at me or one of my men with a gun in your hand," I seethed. "Next time, I'll shove it up your ass and empty the goddamn thing. You got it?"

The man wheezed and struggled for air as I tightened my fingers before finally nodding frantically.

"You see Cyrus Whitlock, you be sure to give him a message from me. There isn't anywhere he can hide that I won't find him." I leaned in closer, baring my teeth, "And when I'm through with him, there won't be a body to find."

With that, I shoved the guy down the stairs and started back to my truck before stopping to point at the cowering dog. "Cut that thing free," I told the man who was still hunched against the side of the house, holding his neck as he pulled in air. That wasn't half as bad as what was done to Serenity. "I come back out here, I better not find him still tied to that goddamn tree. He'd have a better chance out in the wild than he has here."

EIGHTEEN

HUNTER

By the time I pulled up in front of my house, the tenuous hold I'd had on my temper had gotten a little stronger. I could still feel the rage bubbling inside me, but it was more of a simmer than a full, rolling boil.

Just as I killed the engine, the front door opened, back-lighting Lincoln's large figure as he stood in the doorway, arms crossed, feet shoulder-width apart.

He stayed in that position, standing sentry, until I ascended the porch steps. Only then did he step out and close the door behind him.

"She okay?" I asked, tilting my chin up at the front door.

"Out like a light. Has been since her head hit the pillow."

I felt my lungs expand in the first breath of relief I'd

felt all damn night. "Good. Thanks for staying with her," I said as I started past him, reaching for the knob.

He spoke over my shoulder, and what he said froze me to the spot. "Wouldn't have had to if your head hadn't been up your ass."

I slowly turned to look back at my boss, my brother, a man I held great respect for. "What the hell is that supposed to mean?"

He propped his hands on his hips as he glowered.

"You left her alone tonight."

"I needed to take care of something," I bit back, my ire rising at having to explain myself. If anyone could understand what I'd been feeling, it should have been Lincoln. "You were here to keep her safe."

From his darkening expression, that had been the wrong thing to say. "Usually, when a man orders that a woman who's just been attacked will be staying with him in his house, *he's* the one doing the protecting. But instead of doing that, you abandoned her to go off on some insane mission for revenge that isn't even yours to have."

I threw my arm out, pointing in the direction of the living room window. "You see the bruises on her throat?"

"Sure the hell did. But I have to ask, is she your woman?"

Fucking hell. "She's my friend."

His eyes widened and his chin jerked back, sarcasm dripping from his tone as he said, "Is that so? In that case, she would have been just fine staying with her sister and West."

My molars ground together as one thought ran through my head: *Over my dead body.*

"You're a smart man, Hunter. I wouldn't have hired you all those years ago if I'd doubted that for even a second. But the bullshit you pulled tonight, that was just plain stupid. Stupid and fucking reckless. You not only put yourself in danger, but Marco too. And you didn't even stop to think about how what you were doing could affect the prosecution's case when we finally *do* track this motherfucker down. So I feel like I have to ask, is she safe with you? Really and truly safe? Because if you can't get your shit together, I'll take her back with me and work something else out."

The muscles in my neck and back strained tight as everything Lincoln had just said hit home in a really painful way.

He was absolutely right. I'd fucked up, going off the way I had.

I was better than that, but I'd let emotion dictate my actions. That was something that had been trained out of me years ago. The Navy had seen to that, and even if they hadn't, the SEALs certainly did. I should have known better.

Pulling in a steady breath through my nose, I released the fists my hands had been clenched in and flexed my fingers out.

"She's safe with me," I proclaimed. "You have my word. And the shit I pulled tonight won't happen again."

Lincoln took a few seconds to study me; that was just

his way. The man was calm and cool under the tensest circumstances, and he never acted without thought. Finally, he nodded and released his stance. "All right then. I'll leave you to it."

I stood on the porch as he climbed into his own truck, remaining rooted to the spot until his taillights eventually disappeared.

With a heavy sigh, I twisted the knob and threw the door open, only to freeze on the spot the moment I stepped inside, because right there on my couch, fast asleep, was Serenity.

I'd been so laser focused earlier, that I hadn't bothered to stop and think about what I was saying when I'd ordered that she would be staying with me. I hadn't thought about the fact that I only had one bed in the entire house.

The tight ball she was holding herself in in her sleep was like a fist to the chest. She just looked so goddamn tiny and helpless.

I moved closer, pulling that jasmine scent into my lungs. The bruises on her throat looked even worse than they had when I first saw them in the back of the ambulance, so dark and ugly against her creamy alabaster skin.

She'd had one hell of a night, and instead of being able to sleep comfortably, there she was on a fucking couch. Christ, Lincoln was right. I was an asshole.

I moved through the house as silently as possible, locking everything up and turning off all of the lights except for a single standing lamp in the living room, next to the fireplace.

My leg gave a twinge when I crouched to pick Serenity up, but I gritted my teeth and worked through the pain. I'd had that goddamn prosthesis on for too long now, and I was starting to pay for it.

With her scent in my lungs and her weight in my arms, her soft curves molding against me, I carried her into my bedroom and gently placed her in my bed. I watched as she rolled onto her side, giving me her back, and wrapped her arm around one of my pillows, pulling it flush against her on a deep inhale. She snuggled into the mattress once I pulled the covers over her long, creamy legs, and the instant the dark navy sheet settled over her, I was hit with the sensation that she looked right, spread out in the middle of my bed like that. She belonged.

Christ, that wasn't a thought I had any business entertaining.

With a weary sigh, I scrubbed my hands over my face and, as hard as it was, I turned away and softly pulled the door closed behind me, ignoring the voice in my head that screamed at me to just curl up beside her.

Once I was back in the living room, exhaustion from the night overcame me. I barely had the energy to strip down and remove my prosthesis and sleeve before stretching out on the sofa and throwing the blanket Serenity had been using over me.

The pillow beneath my head smelled just like her, and it was on that thought that I closed my eyes and drifted off.

For the first night in weeks, I didn't have nightmares about fire and explosions and pain.

Instead, I dreamed of a honey-haired woman with inquisitive hazel eyes and the most beautiful laugh I'd ever heard.

———

Serenity

I woke up with a jolt, the sound of Cyrus Whitlock's voice and the feel of his hands on my throat yanking me from my sleep.

I pulled in a startled breath and shot up, my muddled brain taking a few beats to reengage and remember. I got away. Cyrus wasn't here. He couldn't get to me. Because I was at Hunter's house.

On that thought, I looked around, my brow knitting in confusion at my surroundings. When I'd fallen asleep, I'd been on Hunter's couch, but that certainly wasn't where I'd woken up.

I tried to find something that might indicate where I was, but there didn't seem to be many personal items lying around, so it was hard to be sure. The most telling thing, however, was the fact that the room was full of Hunter's masculine, intoxicating scent.

It was also surprisingly clean and well put together, given that it was the room of a bachelor.

I wasn't sure what I'd been expecting, maybe a cross between frat boy and middle-aged male living alone, meaning sparsely decorated and messy, but that wasn't the case at all.

The furniture was bold and solidly built, stained a nice, dark color that matched Hunter's personality perfectly. The dark blue sheets I was lying between were soft and warm, and the bedspread on top matched perfectly.

There were beautiful bay windows that had wooden blinds, currently closed against the faint light glowing outside, and above the bed hung a black and white photo that had been blown up and framed. I twisted and scooted across the mattress on my knees to get a better look, and sure enough, it was a picture of Hope Valley, taken, it looked like, from an overlook or cliff somewhere high up in the mountains.

Beside the dresser and a single nightstand, the only other furniture in the room, was a well-worn leather chair and small side table tucked under the windows beside a single bookshelf that was crammed with books.

Curiosity got the best of me, and I threw my legs over the side of the bed, padding quietly to the shelf to get a look.

On the table by the chair was a tattered thriller paper-back with a receipt tucked between the pages as a book-mark. The book looked like it had been read multiple times. As a matter of fact, all the books on the shelf looked well-loved and worn, meaning not only was Hunter an avid reader, but he reread the ones he favored over and over again.

Nature called just then, pulling me from my snooping. Not knowing the time or where Hunter was, I tiptoed to the door and slowly pulled it open so as not to make any noise.

When I didn't see him anywhere in the hall, I quickly shuffled across to the bathroom I'd used the night before and closed myself inside. A quick glance in the mirror had me flinching. The bruises on my throat were even worse this morning than they had been the night before—I didn't have a clue how it was possible for them to have grown even darker overnight, but somehow, they had.

Another thing working against me was my hair. Going to sleep with it wet had been a mistake, because when I pulled the clip out and let the length tumble down my back, it was full of wild, unruly waves.

I tamed it the best I could, then brushed my teeth and washed my face, making sure not to skip the moisturizer this time, before I left the bathroom in search of coffee.

I rounded the corner into the living room and came to a dead stop at the sight of Hunter asleep on the couch.

The breath stalled in my lungs and my mouth dried up as my eyes scanned his body. He was currently stretched out on his back, the flimsy blanket I'd been using the night before was thrown over his lower body, leaving him bare from the waist up. Rippled planes of muscle started at his chest and trailed all the way down his abdomen before disappearing beneath the blanket. He had one arm folded across his stomach, and the other was tossed carelessly over his head, bent at the elbow in a way that accentuated his thick bicep and corded forearm.

He was a freaking Adonis. His likeness should have been carved from marble and put in a museum somewhere.

I licked my lips as my eyes dipped lower, taking in those sexy-as-hell muscles that formed a V at his hips, like a damn arrow pointing to the promised land.

But that was where my perusal ended, because I noticed something propped against the coffee table in front of the couch that made me pause.

I tiptoed closer for a better look and sucked in a breath when I finally realized what it was. All of a sudden, so many things about Hunter started to make sense, from the slight hitch in his gait to the shadows that lingered in his eyes. I could only imagine what had happened to cause the loss of his leg.

It couldn't have been something from his childhood, because he'd been in the military for years. My gut told me that this was the cause of his retirement from the SEALs, and that knowledge made me incredibly sad.

"You know, it won't jump up and kick you," he said, giving me a little start.

My gaze ripped off the prosthetic leg and shot up to his icy blues, glassy with sleep and somewhat guarded as he lay there, studying my expression.

"Then you got ripped off," I said, unsure of where the words were coming from, but unable to stop them nonetheless. "I heard the newfangled ones will even dance a little jig for you."

His eyes widened for just a second before a bark of flabbergasted laugher burst from his throat.

"Gotta say, Wildcat, I didn't expect that kind of reaction. Usually when people find out I'm missing half a leg, I either get pity or unbridled curiosity. A time or two there was even a bit of disgust."

For crying out loud, people really were the worst sometimes.

I shrugged. "Do you want my pity?"

His gaze went hard as he sat up and twisted, throwing his legs over the side and tossing the blanket back to give me a clear view. Sure enough, the left one had been amputated a couple inches below the knee. When I lifted my gaze back to his, he was waiting, scrutinizing to see if there was disgust. He wasn't going to get that kind of reaction from me.

"Not even a little."

"Do you want me to ask you a bunch of invasive, personal questions?"

He hooked a single eyebrow up. "Can it wait until after coffee?"

NINETEEN
SERENITY

A raw giggle pushed its way up my throat, but I held back the wince when I saw how the raspy sound made his eyes darken dangerously.

"Definitely after coffee," I spoke, pulling his head from the dark path I could see his thoughts start to travel.

He blinked, and the storm clouds that had been threatening were gone. "Deal. Can you do me a favor and grab the crutch from the hall closet? Second door on the left."

"Yeah, sure." I hustled down the hallway and pulled open the door he indicated. When I returned to the living room, he was already standing, and I nearly swallowed my tongue at the sight of him in nothing but snug, black boxer briefs.

I was snapped back from my ogling when he cleared his throat. "Oh, uh . . ." I thrust the crutch out to him. "Here you go."

He took it with a chuckle that warmed me from the inside out and tucked it under his left arm, using it to help him navigate his way to the kitchen.

I followed after him, noticing his back for the first time. There were scars all across his torso I hadn't noticed before, spanning across his shoulders and running in a jagged, diagonal line down to his right hip. The man's body looked like it could have been sculpted from stone, but his flesh told a dark story that made my heart clench painfully in my chest.

I did my best not to stare as I hopped up on one of the barstools across the counter from him. Scars or not, Hunter McCann was still the most gorgeous man I'd ever laid eyes on. If anything, seeing what he'd survived made the pull I felt to him even stronger.

From the ease in which he moved around the kitchen preparing the coffee machine, it was obvious he was used to the crutch. But my curiosity had gotten the best of me.

"How come you didn't put the prosthesis back on?" I asked, propping my chin in my hand."

Once the coffee was brewing, he moved to another cabinet and pulled out a medicine bottle. "I kept it on for too long yesterday. Overdid it a bit, so I'm paying for that this morning." He dumped a couple capsules into his hand, and I recognized them as over-the-counter pain meds. "Once these kick in, I'll be good to go. Until then, I'm giving my leg a break."

He threw the pills back before turning to face me, his

eyes once more traveling to my throat. "How are you feeling this morning?"

I sat up straight, lifting my fingers to the side of my neck to brush across my skin. That barely-there pressure was still enough to make me flinch and draw my hand away. While the outside was black and blue, the inside felt swollen and bruised, and my voice still hadn't returned to normal.

"Well, I don't think I'll be singing at the Tap Room any time soon," I attempted to joke, but it fell flat. "I really am okay, Hunter," I professed when his lips flattened into an unamused line. "He scared me, and he hurt me, but I made sure he got his too." I held up my nails as I remembered the blood I'd drawn. "You should have seen the claw marks I left on that asshole's face."

The coffee maker gurgled as the last of the rich, dark brew dripped into the carafe. Hunter moved to the cabinet above and pulled down two cups, filling them both before bringing one over and setting it in front of me. He went back for his as he said, "Milk's in the fridge and sugar's on the counter if you want it."

"Thanks." I hopped off the barstool and headed to the fridge to doctor my coffee the way I liked it. When I spun back around, I noticed his gaze was pointed where my ass had just been.

Heat rushed to my cheeks at the hungry look in his eyes, and it was all I could do not to melt into a puddle right there on the floor. I sat back on the stool and cast my eyes down as I took my first sip while butterflies burst to life in my belly.

A minute later, Hunter spoke, breaking through the tension that was starting to fill the air. "I'm proud of you for fighting back, sweetheart. But I want to put my fist through something every time I look up and see those bruises."

This was just another reason my head was so muddled when it came to this man. Friends were protective of each other, sure, but this was next level. When he took off last night, I was scared he was going to kill someone. He went further than even my father and brother had with his rage. I was trying to respect the line he'd drawn weeks ago after that first kiss, but it was getting harder and harder.

"Bruises fade, Hunter." I let my eyes travel over his body to his leg. "I think you know that, honey. You can't go around shoving your fist through stuff when you get pissed off."

He inhaled deeply, dragging a breath in through his nose. Those icy blue eyes kept me pinned in place as he lifted the mug to his lips and took a drink. Why wasn't I surprised to learn the man took his coffee black?

"All right. I promise I'll do everything in my power to keep my cool."

I smiled, feeling better than I had since I got home from my first ever girls' night and had everything go epically sideways. "I appreciate that. Now, as a thank you for letting me have your bed last night, I'm going to make you breakfast," I announced, hopping off the stool and moving back to the fridge. "Seeing as you're a guy, I'm hoping you have bacon."

"In the crisper drawer on the left," he instructed.

"Aha!" I pulled the bacon out and foraged for everything else I'd need to make a simple breakfast of eggs, bacon, and toast. "You're on toast duty," I said as I spun around and deposited everything on the island. "Think you can handle that?"

One corner of his mouth hooked up in a crooked smirk. "I think that's within my skill set."

We lapsed into a comfortable routine. I cooked as he got out plates and silverware and set them on the island for us to eat at.

The conversation was easy, like both of us were mindful to stay away from the heavier topics. I was curious to ask how he'd lost his leg, but I got the impression that particular topic made him tense. I didn't blame him one damn bit. I was sure the story came with some pretty terrible memories. And I could be patient. I'd wait for him to tell me when he was ready, and if that day never came, I was okay with that too.

I loaded our plates while he poured two glasses of orange juice, then we sat side by side and dug in.

"Thanks, Wildcat. This is great."

I shrugged as I swallowed down the bite I'd just taken. "It's no big deal. I like to cook."

I lifted my orange juice and took a sip when something from the corner of my eye caught my attention. I read the fancy script and lifted my brows. "Ooh, you have a wedding next weekend? Fun."

He crunched into a strip of bacon and let out a grunt that sounded less than enthusiastic.

I bit off the corner of my toast. "You're not looking forward to it?"

"Not particularly."

I dusted the crumbs off my hand and twisted on the stool to face him fully.

He swallowed a bite of eggs and regarded me curiously. "What? Why are you looking at me like that?"

"You're a grump."

He choked on the sip of coffee he'd just taken and coughed. "What?"

"You're a grump," I repeated on a laugh. "You don't like engagement parties or weddings, and you get all grunty and grumbly when talking about either. It's like you turn into a seventy-year-old man."

"I do not," he said, affronted, his brows knitting together in a frown.

I poked my finger into the divot between his eyebrows. "You do too. Weddings are awesome. You should be excited."

He rolled his eyes on another grunt.

I snatched up the invitation and scanned the script. "So, who is Vera Moss and Oliver James?"

His chest heaved on an inhale. The energy in the room started to shift, the air sparking and crackling. He cleared his throat like he was suddenly uncomfortable, and when he spoke, he faced forward, like he was unable to look at me.

"Vera was married to a buddy of mine from my old team."

I tilted my head to the side. "Team?"

"SEAL team," he explained. Then what he said next was like a punch to the chest. "We lost him in the same explosion that took my leg."

I sucked in a gasp that made my throat throb. "Hunter," I whispered, my voice pained.

He continued on like he hadn't heard me, and given the shadows that cast over his features, I thought maybe he hadn't, being too lost in the memories of the past. "It was just a goddamn kid. We saw him coming but didn't think he was a threat." He shook his head in disgust and repeated, "A fucking kid."

"Hunter, you don't have to—"

"He pulled out a fucking launcher and fired an RPG into the building where we'd set up camp. Bryce and I lost Moss and Danielson, another member of our team, and I lost my goddamn leg. Vera is Moss's widow. She's getting remarried to this Oliver guy."

More than anything, I wanted to lean in and give him a hug, but something told me he wouldn't appreciate that, so I forced myself to hold back.

His eyes looked haunted as he spoke, and it was killing me to see him go from the easy-going guy he'd been only minutes ago, back to the gruff, stormy man I'd first met.

"Hunter," I said in a quiet voice. When his eyes came

to me, I pulled in a deep breath at the shadows dancing in them. "I'm sorry I brought it up."

The corners of his mouth tipped up in a small, sad grin. "It's alright, sweetheart. Not like you knew."

"I can see why you might not be excited to go."

He grunted in response before sucking back the last of his juice like he wished it was a shot of tequila or something. "Yeah, well, I almost didn't. But she's got two boys, Luke and Liam. We're tight. After I was discharged from the hospital, I came back and spent the next few years trying to make up for the loss of their dad. They're the closest thing I have to my own flesh and blood. I gave them my word I'd go, so . . ." he trailed off on a shrug. Just when I thought I couldn't possibly be more drawn to this man than I already was, he went and said something that made me weak in the knees. He really was the best man I'd ever met.

"I'll go with you," I blurted out, the words falling past my lips before I could give it a single thought.

He turned to look at me in bewilderment. "What?"

A part of me wished I could rewind time and edit that last part out, but since I couldn't I decided to just ride the wave I'd put into motion. "I'll go with you. You're clearly not looking forward to this wedding, which means you'll probably end up miserable the whole time. I love weddings. They're an excuse to eat great food, dance until you're exhausted, and, fingers crossed, enjoy the open bar. That's my kind of party. So, instead of you going by yourself and being bored out of your mind, I'll be your platonic date, and I'll show you what all the hype is about."

He didn't look convinced, but I hated the idea of him being miserable, so I sweetened the deal. "And you haven't even seen me do the chicken dance. You're in for a real treat, my friend."

His brow furrowed, the corners of his mouth dancing with a suppressed grin. "You're serious."

"Hell yeah!" I exclaimed excitedly. "And this will give me an excuse to buy a hot new dress and killer shoes. It's a win-win. So what do you say?" I leaned in and bumped my shoulder against his. "You want to take me along with you so I can show you what all the hype is really about?"

Finally, the smile he'd been holding back broke free, and damn if it didn't make me want to climb him like a tree. Not necessarily the "friendliest" thought, but who could blame me when he was sitting there looking so damn sexy?

"All right. You have a deal."

I did an excited little shimmy in my seat and threw my arms in the air. "You won't regret it," I promised before hopping off the stool. "I'm going to grab a quick shower. Since I cooked, you're on cleanup duty. Chop, chop, little onion."

He looked at me with wide, flabbergasted eyes. "You can't be serious?" he called as I started out of the kitchen.

"Oh, I'm dead serious," I said over my shoulder as I moved down the hall. "And don't think you'll get any sympathy points or con your way out of it because you've only got one leg, buddy. I've seen your muscles. You can obviously do more with one leg than most men can with two."

I shut the bathroom door on his burst of laughter, and despite the hellacious night before, I spent the rest of the morning smiling. Because earning Hunter's laughter felt like a gift.

TWENTY
SERENITY

It had been three days since the incident at my apartment, and as much as I appreciated Hunter going out of his way to take care of me, I was quickly starting to lose my mind.

I'd never been the kind of person who could just sit still, but that was all I'd been doing since being dropped off at his house, and I was going stir crazy.

Rory had given me the week off with orders not to worry about coming in to work until I was fully healed. While all I wanted to do was get back to my normal life, I understood where she was coming from. Fletcher didn't need to see me like this. We were doing what we could to keep the events of that night from him, because I knew he would blame himself for what his father had done, and it wasn't his fault. He already carried too much on his shoulders because of that man. I wasn't going to add to that weight. If anything, I desperately wanted to lighten the burden for him.

What I hadn't realized the night Hunter demanded I be delivered to his house, was that any sense of freedom I had before had disappeared.

I appreciated everything he had done for me, but if I'd known I was losing all sense of privacy, I would have put up a bigger fight.

Hunter went out of his way to make me feel comfortable, and had even gone so far as to work from home the past couple of days. But a case he had at Alpha Omega required his attention, so he had to go into the office earlier that morning. I could see the hesitance on his face when it came time for him to leave, and I assured him I'd be okay on my own. But right before he walked out the door, he informed me that I wasn't to leave his house without an escort.

My eyes went big, threatening to fall right out of my skull. "You've got to be kidding me," I exclaimed.

He stood at the door, dressed in another pair of distressed jeans, and an old, faded T-shirt, looking like delicious sin. Feet braced shoulder-width apart and arms crossed over his chest, he scowled at me like I was a petulant child. "Far from kidding, Wildcat. You plan to leave this house, you have someone with you at all times. I don't want you by yourself until that son of a bitch has been arrested."

I threw my arms up in exasperation before letting them flop back down and slap against my hips. Leo and

Micah had done what they could to keep me informed of the investigation, but so far there had been no sign of Cyrus Whitlock anywhere. His neighbors reported he hadn't returned to his home, and there'd been no sign of his car anywhere. There was an APB or BOLO or some other cop acronym out on the guy, but so far, they'd turned up a whole lot of nothing.

The man had disappeared into the wind, and because of that I was the one paying for it.

"I think I've proven I'm more than capable of taking care of myself," I demanded, bracing my hands on my hips and giving him just as a severe look as he was giving me. "You can't just keep me in this house all day every day."

Those unfathomable eyes pinned me in place. "The hell I can't," he clipped angrily. "Until I'm sure you're safe, I'm not taking any risks. You matter to me, Sere."

Damn it, he wasn't playing fair, and at that confession, the wind effectively went out of my sails. I let out a pained groan and dropped my head back, feeling the tension start to throb behind my temples.

Sensing I was at my wits' end, Hunter moved to me, placing his hands on my arms gently, until I lifted my head and looked at him. The lines in the corners of his eyes creased deeper with concern, and his brow furrowed. "I'm not trying to take away your freedom. I just need to keep you safe. Can you let me do that? Please."

The hint of desperation in his tone tugged at my chest, and I couldn't bring myself to deny him. How was I supposed to when everything he was doing was solely to keep me safe?

As if sensing me wavering, one side of his mouth hooked up in a small smirk. "I'm not saying you have to stay here forever. You can leave whenever you want. All I'm asking is you take someone with you. Can you give me that, sweetheart? Just for my peace of mind?"

He knew he was winning, and he was pulling out all the stops to get his way. I scowled, clenching my fists at my side, but there was no heat behind my glare.

"Fine," I relented. Goosebumps broke out across my skin as he slid those work-roughened hands down my arms and wrapped his long fingers around my wrists. The touch was gentle, meant to give comfort, but it sparked something deep inside me that only grew hotter.

"Thank you, baby," he said quietly.

If it hadn't been for his hold on me, that one word, spoken so tenderly, would have made my knees weak. I'd never gotten that from him before. I got *sweetheart* and *Wildcat*, both of which made my insides quiver. But that was my first *baby*, and damn, but I loved it.

That was how I came to be sitting in a booth at Evergreen Diner across from Stella and Sage.

I had to get out of the house. I hadn't been able to take it for another second, so in my desperation, I'd called my sister and informed her, if she didn't get me the hell out of here, I was executing a jail break.

My voice was finally back to normal, and the bruises had lightened enough that I was able to cover them with a healthy bit of concealer, so when Stella told me she was coming to my rescue, I darted to the guest bathroom I'd taken over in the days I'd been here and got to work.

She and Sage had shown up twenty minutes later in Sage's fine-as-hell classic black Mustang. If I hadn't loved her so much, I might have pushed her down a well so I could steal it and take it for a joy ride across the country.

Happy with the job I'd done with the cover-up, I skipped out of the house, feeling like I was floating on air. It was pathetic, really, how excited I was for a trip to the local diner. But I was sick and tired of my own company. I was ready to be around other people.

Silence fell over our table as I scanned the menu, trying to decide what I wanted to eat. It was always a difficult task, seeing as everything Ralph cooked was delicious. I was bouncing between the country fried steak sandwich and the turkey club, trying to pick, when Stella cleared her throat.

I glanced up, noticing for the first time that neither of them focused on their menus, but instead, were staring across the table at me like I was some sort of science experiment.

I arched a single brow, my gaze ping-ponging between the two of them. "Uh, can I help you?"

Sage looked to my sister and shook her head. "See? I told you she wouldn't spill."

"What?"

They both ignored me. Stella rolled her eyes. "It's

barely been five minutes. Just give her some time, would you? Be patient."

Sage blew out a raspberry. "Please. You know me well enough to know patience most certainly *isn't* a virtue of mine."

What the hell was going on?

"Uh, hello!" I called loudly, leaning in to wave my hand in their faces. "It's not nice to talk about me like I'm not here, so someone better spill before I lose my freaking mind."

Before either of them could say a word, Sally came to a stop at the end of our table.

"She spilled the beans yet?"

"No." Sage and Stella answered at the same time.

I threw my hands in the air. "For the love of God! Will someone tell me what the hell is going on?"

Stella let out a deep breath and met my gaze, biting her bottom lip before she finally announced, "There's kind of a town-wide bet going on right now."

My chin jerked back in confusion. "A bet? What kind of bet?"

Sally was the one to answer. "A bet for when you and that fine hunk of man you're currently shacked up with finally get together."

I'd made the mistake of lifting my water glass and taking a sip as she spoke, and the moment she finished her sentence, the sip I took went down the wrong pipe, and I began to choke.

I keeled over, coughing violently as I tried to clear my airway.

"The hell is goin' on out there?" Ralph bellowed, his big, bearded face popping up through the passthrough window.

"Nothin'," Sally shouted back. That was kind of their thing. They were known far and wide for hilariously hollering the diner down. Most everyone who stepped foot in the place came not only because the food was delicious, but also for the free show. "Serenity's just chokin' a little bit. Mind your damn business and get back to cooking. We got hungry mouths to feed out here."

"Sere girl is here?" Ralph asked, ignoring his wife's order. "You ask her yet if her and her man have banged it out yet?"

Good God!

"Hunter and I are *not* banging it out," I declared loudly, and through the blood rushing in my ears, I could have sworn I heard several grumbles of displeasure from the people sitting at the tables around us.

I whipped around and pinned my sister with wide-eyed shock. "You're telling me there's a town-wide bet on when Hunter and I are going to have sex?" I squeaked shrilly. Thank God my voice had healed, or that noise coming from my throat would have seriously hurt.

My sister had the good grace to wince at my question, but it was Sage who answered. "Not exactly when you'll have sex, more like when you two finally get together."

"My money's on a week from tomorrow, so if you

could hold out a little longer, I'd be more than grateful," Sally declared.

"Woman," Ralph bellowed from the kitchen. "You better not be connivin' out there! You wanna win, you have to do it fair and square!"

A headache that hadn't been there thirty seconds ago popped up behind my eyeballs.

"If it makes you feel better," Sage began to explain, "this is somewhat of a Hope Valley tradition. People have been betting on relationships since before I moved to town. There was even a pool on when Hayden and Micah would get together."

"Lost myself a cool hundred on that one!" Ralph shouted, and I had to admit, I was starting to find the whole thing kind of funny.

"With Hunter bein' the last bachelor standin', the competition is fierce," Sally declared. "And with you stayin' at his house and all, jaws are waggin'."

"There's nothing for them to wag about. There's nothing going on between Hunter and me. We're just friends," I insisted vehemently, ignoring the sour, acrid taste that statement left on my tongue.

It was the truth, damn it. But what I was keeping to myself, what I refused to share with anyone, including my sister, was the fact that I was steadily and quickly falling for the man.

I'd had my heart shattered once before by a man I thought was going to be the love of my life. I'd been convinced he was *The One*. Capital letters and everything.

I was so certain he loved me for me, that I convinced myself he would accept the truth about me and my family, warts and all.

At the time, I'd refused to pull honey traps, because it felt like cheating, but I'd still run cons, considering it was all I'd ever known.

Man, had I been wrong. Not only had he kicked me to the curb the moment he learned the truth about my family, but he'd also told all of our friends, so when I lost him, I lost everyone.

But what I'd felt for him was nothing compared to the way Hunter made me feel. That heartache had wrecked me. It was terrifying to know that Hunter not only had the power to break my heart, but also to shatter my world. If things went badly, I knew I wouldn't survive it.

"Just friends, my old wrinkled behind," a voice from behind me declared, and when I turned around, I saw Ms. McClintock, the blue-haired blunt-as-hell octogenarian who ran around town, stirring up trouble and spreading gossip far and wide.

"Seen the way that boy looks at you, and if that's the look of friendship, I'm goin' blind *and* senile."

It was kind of hilarious to hear her refer to Hunter as a boy, given he was in his early forties.

"Ms. M," I started to object, but she slashed a hand through the air and cut me off.

"You listen here, girly," she said, pointing a gnarled, arthritic finger in my face. "I've lost more money on the youngsters in this town than I care to admit, and I'll be damned if I lose the pool on the last of them Alpha Omega men. Now, you do what I say and take yourself back home, douse yourself in whatever perfume you kids are wearin' now-a-days, put on your skimpiest undies, and seduce that big lump of muscle into winnin' me my money back!"

My mouth had fallen open in complete shock. Hell, the entire diner had lapsed into silence at her order.

All I could do was sit there, gaping up at the old lady and nod.

"Good," she clipped. "My work here is done." She started out of the diner but stopped to proclaim over her shoulder. "I'll see you at the Tap Room next Friday. And I expect to see you back up on that stage, singin' your lungs out, now that you're healed up."

And with that, she was gone.

I slowly swiveled back around in my seat, blinking slowly. "Can someone tell me what just happened?"

Stella was too busy giggling to get a word in edgewise, so Sage took it upon herself to speak. "Welcome to Hope Valley, honey. Where the men are gorgeous and the crazy is in abundance."

She had that right.

TWENTY-ONE
HUNTER

I was dead on my feet.

Sleeping three nights on a couch that was too damn soft and not nearly long or wide enough would do that to a man, but as long as the threat of Cyrus Whitlock was still out there, I'd suck it up and deal. Keeping Serenity safe was worth any amount of discomfort, and I'd dealt with a whole hell of a lot more in my lifetime. This was nothing.

Leaning back in my chair, I closed my eyes and scrubbed at my face, the words on the computer screen starting to blur together.

She had texted me when her sister and Sage showed to pick her up for lunch, and again when she got back home, but I kept checking my phone damn near constantly since then, hoping for another message from her.

It wasn't rational, and I knew I was the one who put us in the place we were currently in, but I missed her when she wasn't around. There was just something about her, a light, like the sun breaking through storm clouds after the heavy rain. She made me laugh more than I had in longer than I cared to admit. When I was with her, it was easy to forget the bad. The nightmares came with less frequency, and I felt the desire to smile.

I tapped the screen on my phone, bringing it to life for the fifth time in less than three minutes and feeling my stomach sink when there was no message light.

It was barely five o'clock, and usually I would've worked for at least another hour, but the desire to get home was overwhelming. I kept telling myself it was because I was tired, but the truth was, I wanted to walk through my front door and see her smiling face look over at me from whatever she was doing the moment I appeared. That damn smile was the best welcome home greeting I'd had.

I was just starting to shut down my computer when Bryce popped up in my open doorway, leaning his shoulder against the door frame and crossing his arms over his chest.

"So you want to tell me what the hell is going on, or should I get my news through the town grapevine?"

I felt my forehead pull into a frown. "Am I supposed to know what the hell you're talking about?"

He gave me a look that said he knew I was full of shit. "About you and Serenity," he stated. "Town's got another pool going on to see when you two will end up together. You feel like telling me where I should put my money?"

I felt my back go straight as I studied his features to see if he was pulling my leg. When it became obvious he wasn't, I let out a huff of air and collapsed back in my chair.

"It's not like that," I insisted. But even though I had said the words a million times, they were starting to feel like a lie on my tongue. "She's just staying with me until that fucker is off the streets. I'm only keeping her safe."

I knew I wasn't fooling him. If one person on the face of the earth knew me best, it was the man standing right in front of me.

"And you mean to tell me there wasn't a soul in all of Hope Valley who couldn't have protected her just as capably as you? Say, your buddy West, for instance? You know, the man who's about to be her brother-in-law. You don't think he'd be able to look after her?"

I opened my mouth to respond but had nothing. "You finished?" I finally asked, my hackles rising. "'Cause I'd like to get home if it's all the same to you."

The expression on Bryce's face shifted then. He was the kind of man who hid behind a carefree façade. He pretended not to give a damn, but deep down, there wasn't much he didn't see, and I knew by the way he was looking at me, he wasn't anywhere near done.

"Tell me, who were you hoping to hear from when you checked your phone just a moment ago?" *Son of a bitch.* "Or any of the other million times you've checked it the past few days?"

"You're way off the mark," I grunted, but the truth was, he'd just hit the nail on the goddamn head.

"What are you doing, man?" he finally asked, cutting to the root of things. "You moved her in, refusing to let anyone else look after her but you. You're taking her to Vera's wedding, for Christ's sake. Have you given a single goddamn thought to what your actions might look like to her?"

"I've been up front with her from the beginning. We're just friends. She knows that."

"She knows that's what you *said*," he stressed. "But then you go and do shit that a man who's just friends with a woman wouldn't do. Hell, man. Even I'm questioning how you feel about her."

My hands clenched tight. "This is none of your business."

He shrugged. "Maybe. Maybe not. Way I see it, this is payback for forcing me to pull my head out of my ass when it came to Tessa. I'm just returning the favor."

"Bryce—"

"She's good for you," he said, cutting off my argument. "Whether you see it or not, everyone else around here does. You were turning into a miserable asshole. Only one worse than you was Xander, and that's saying something, man. But lately, you've been in a better mood. You're cutting up again, laughing more."

"You grow a vagina when no one was looking?" I snapped, using sarcasm to deflect.

"If there's a woman out there who's a better match for

you, I've never met her. I like Serenity for you, brother. And what's more, I think if you got your head out of *your* ass, you'd feel the same way."

With that last well-placed blow hitting his mark, he pushed off the doorframe, turned on his boot, and walked away, leaving me reeling.

———

Serenity

I'd been antsy since my sister and Sage dropped me off back at Hunter's place a few hours ago. I tried watching television, but nothing held my interest. I even tried reading one of Hunter's thrillers, but when I got to the part where the bad guy was slinking into the protagonist's bedroom window, I started to get creeped out. The story was hitting a little too close to home, given my current situation, so I slapped the book closed and tossed it onto the coffee table with a huff of annoyance.

Finally, I decided that cooking would be the best way to pull me out of my funk, so I headed for Hunter's kitchen. I noticed that first morning that he only had the bare minimum in his fridge and pantry, and seeing as I wasn't a big fan of protein bars and smoothies, I'd written out an extensive list and made him go to the grocery store with the order that he wasn't allowed to come back unless he bought every single item.

Needless to say, I had everything I could possibly need to cook whatever my heart desired, so I'd decided on homemade lasagna with sauce made from scratch, fresh garlic bread, and a salad.

The sauce was a recipe I'd gotten from my mom who got it from her mom, and so on, but I'd always loved to experiment with flavors, so I'd played with it over the years and made something already delicious that much better.

I'd always enjoyed cooking. Food was a big deal in my family. Sunday dinners were a regular thing with us, and unless you had a damn good excuse—say, getting choked out by a demented psycho—you were expected to be there. I could count on one hand the number of Sunday dinners I'd missed. It was the only time I got to flex my cooking muscles. I'd head over to my parents' house early so I could help my mom in the kitchen.

Back when I'd been with my ex, I'd gone out of my way to make him dinner as often as I could, but then we broke up, and cooking for one didn't hold nearly the same appeal. I knew this whole situation with Hunter was temporary, and I'd probably be heading back to my apartment sooner rather than later, but I planned to take advantage of it while I could.

The lasagna was done and in the oven with the garlic bread to keep warm, and the salad was prepared and in the fridge to keep from wilting. The house was filled with the smells of dinner, making my stomach rumble as I washed and dried the dishes I used to make dinner. I had music streaming from my phone as I moved around the kitchen, mindlessly singing along with whatever song was playing at the time, and that was how Hunter found me only a few minutes after everything was done.

I'd just spun around from putting the silverware away when I spotted him standing in the entryway of the kitchen.

He gave me a start, causing me to jump. "You know, for a guy your size, you're shockingly quiet." I let out a laugh and placed a hand over my chest to soothe my racing heart. "You damn near gave me a heart attack."

"Sorry about that," he said with the smallest of smirks. "Didn't mean to scare you."

I waved him off. "It's fine. I just didn't expect you for a bit longer. But, surprise," I exclaimed, holding my arms out wide, "I made dinner."

There was something in his blue eyes I couldn't quite put my finger on, but as he moved closer, it flickered and flashed like fire. "I figured that from the smells."

I cocked a brow. "Good smells or bad smells?" I asked teasingly, because I already knew the answer. Not to toot my own horn or anything, but I was a fantastic cook.

He was still moving in my direction as he said, "Fucking *incredible* smells," on a deep, raspy growl.

My breath caught at the deep timbre of his voice and the almost predatory way he watched me as he slowly moved closer. I suddenly felt as though I was prey being stalked by a much bigger, stronger animal.

"Uh . . ." I took a step back, grabbing hold of the counter for balance when I nearly tripped over my own feet. There had only been one time in our acquaintance when Hunter had looked at me the way he was just then, and that had been the night we kissed.

You're reading too much into things, Serenity, I silently scolded. I needed to get my shit together before I did something incredibly stupid. *Again.*

"Well, I hope you're hungry." Shaking myself out of my stupor, I grabbed the oven mitts from where I'd tossed them on the island earlier, and spun around to pull the door down. "I kind of made a lot," I said as I reached in and pulled out the tray of lasagna. "I cut the recipe in half since it's just the two of us, but it still made quite a bit. I figured you could take the leftovers into the office with you, maybe pawn them off on some of the other guys."

I was rambling, but I couldn't get my brain and mouth on the same page.

Hunter stopped only inches away from me as I carefully placed the tray on the island. He was so damn close, I could smell his cologne over the food. I wasn't sure if the heat spreading over me just then was from the oven still being open, or because he was *right there.*

"Um, c-could you grab the garlic bread and slice it while I get the salad?" I asked, my voice coming out wobbly.

"Sure thing, baby."

Oh damn. I got another baby. I didn't know what was happening or why Hunter's mood felt different. All I knew was he was confusing the hell out of me, and it was really starting to piss me off.

While he unwrapped the foil from the bread and cut into its flaky crust, I kept my hands busy doing everything else. I placed the salad bowl on the island, then moved to the cupboard for plates. I lifted up on my tiptoes to grab glasses when Hunter's heat returned.

"I've got it, sweetheart," he said as he came up behind me. My lungs seized when he pressed his chest into my back and braced one hand on my hip while he reached up with the other to pull two glasses down.

I could feel him *everywhere*, and those hard planes of muscle pressing against me sent a rush of arousal into my blood. My core began to throb, and I had to bite my bottom lip to keep from whimpering as the noticeable bulge behind his fly pressed into my back.

I was quickly coming undone.

"Hunter," I breathed, bracing my hands on the countertop in front of me and closing my eyes.

He lowered his arms, setting the glasses down beside my right hand, but didn't move away.

"Yeah, Sere?"

I swallowed past the dryness in my throat. "What is this?"

At my question, he caged me in, brushing the hair away from my neck so I could feel his lips whisper across the tender skin as he said, "This is me finally deciding I'm done fighting what I feel for you, because I want you so goddamn bad I can't see straight."

And on those words, I snapped.

Twenty-Two
Hunter

She whipped around, all that sun-kissed hair flying wild before I got those gorgeous hazel eyes that made me hard as stone and threw my world off its axis.

I wasn't sure how I'd expected her to react to my brutal honesty, but I didn't hesitate to react when she closed the last of the infinitesimal space between us and threw her arms around my neck. The moment her lips crashed against mine, I took complete control. This was the second time she'd initiated a kiss between us, and I wasn't going to make the same fucking mistake I made last time and freeze up.

Instead, I fisted a hand in her hair, wrapped an arm around her waist, and spun her around so I could shove her up against the kitchen island as I feasted from her mouth like a man having his first meal after a month in the desert.

A tiny whimper slipped up her throat, and I quickly swallowed it down, the delicate, beautiful sound making my dick throb and pulse behind my fly.

Christ, I fucking wanted her. When I walked in here tonight to all those delicious smells of a home cooked meal, I thought she couldn't possibly get any better. Then I stepped into the entryway of the kitchen and saw her. Her hips were swaying in the most seductive, transfixing way as she moved around the space, and the soft sound of her voice as she quietly sang along to the song playing from her phone hit me right in the gut, nearly knocking the air from my lungs.

She hadn't heard me come in, giving me those few precious moments of seeing her raw and unfiltered. Then she hit me with that smile, and I was done for.

Never in my life had I had someone to come home to, someone who was *happy* to see me at the end of a long day, and I didn't realize until Bryce pointed it out, that I got exactly that from Serenity Ryan, and I was quickly becoming addicted to it.

She saw me. *All* of me. And it wasn't just for show. I knew that days ago when she made the crack about not using my lack of two legs as a way to get out of cleaning up.

I'd admit that I pushed her that first morning to see how she'd react. I didn't usually walk around my house in my underwear when I had company, but I wanted to see what the sight of my scars would do. How she'd handle seeing all the damage that had been done to my body.

She hadn't even flinched. In fact, she'd even voiced her appreciation for my body. If I were being honest with myself—something I hadn't done in quite a while—that had been a turning point between us. One that I'd insisted on fighting until Bryce knocked some sense into me earlier.

"Jesus," I grunted as I pulled at her hair, forcing her head back so I could drag my lips across her throat, peppering those fading bruises with kisses as I ground my hips against her. "Never been this hard in my life."

She moaned wantonly as she reached down with one hand and dug her nails into my ass through my jeans, pulling me harder against her. "Hunter," she panted as she blinked her eyes open, her irises dark as night and brimming with lust. "I need you."

I wasn't sure three words had ever caused such a visceral reaction before. It was only by the grace of God that I didn't come right then and there.

"You need me to make you come?" I teased, biting down on her bottom lip before dragging my tongue across it to soothe the sting.

A wicked smile tipped her lips up. It was one I'd never seen from her before, and fuck me, but it set my blood on fire, because with that smile, she'd changed the game.

"No, baby. I need to taste you."

She caught me off guard with her statement—just enough to push me off balance. She used that to her advantage and shoved me back two steps until my hips crashed into the counter behind me. Then she nearly made me swallow my tongue when she dropped to her knees right there in front of me.

I barely had time to brace my hands against the edge before she worked my jeans open and was pulling my solid length free. I was so hard I could feel my heartbeat in my cock as precum dripped from the head.

Looking up at me through the thick fringe of her long lashes, she let out an appreciative hum and licked her lips like she was starving, and only my cock could sate her.

It was then that I realized my nickname for her worked in more than one way. Goddamn Wildcat.

"Like what you see?" I rasped, the muscles in my jaw clenching tighter as I white-knuckled the counter.

She didn't hesitate to answer. "Most beautiful cock I've ever seen." Then she opened her mouth, that soft pink tongue of hers poked out, and she swiped the ejaculate that was dripping from the crown.

If I hadn't been leaning against the counter, my knees would have buckled right then and there. As it was, a string of curses blasted past my lips as she wrapped hers around my cock and sucked me deep into her mouth.

"Fucking, *Christ*," I grunted, reaching out with one hand to wrap her hair around my fist so I could see her more clearly. "You look so fucking hot like this, with my dick stretching your mouth wide."

She let out a hum I felt in my balls and spine before swallowing, taking me so deep I bumped the back of her throat.

"Goddamn it, Sere," I hissed. "Feels too good, baby. Don't know how much longer I can hold it."

She released me with a loud pop, dragging her tongue over her swollen lips like she couldn't get enough of my taste. "Then don't hold back. I want you to lose control."

I wanted that too, but not until I was buried as deep inside her pussy as I could possibly get.

Reaching down, I grabbed her under her arms and hauled her up, nearly laughing at the sight of her pout as she exclaimed, "I wasn't finished with that."

Jesus, she was fucking perfect.

"Baby, you want me to come down your throat, I'm game, anytime. Just not the first time I have you. When I come, it's gonna be with my cock inside you and we're gonna do it together."

Her eyelids went half-mast at my declaration, her chest rising and falling on a quick breath. Yeah, she was down for my plan.

Reaching for the hem of her shirt, I pulled it up and over her head before tossing it over my shoulder, leaving her in nothing but a flimsy pair of leggings that made her ass look downright bitable and a pale pink bra, covered in lace.

"Tell me something, Sere," I started as I dragged one hand up the dip in her waist, memorizing her sweet curves as I stopped at her perfect tits. I pulled one lacy cup down and dragged my thumb across the stiff peak of her rosy pink nipple, making it pucker even tighter. Everything about her was beautiful. "Did sucking me off like that make you wet?"

She let out a tiny whimper before releasing her bottom lip from between her teeth and issuing a challenge that set my blood on fire.

"Why don't you see for yourself."

I didn't hesitate. I shoved my hand down the front of her leggings only to discover she wasn't wearing any panties. "Dirty girl," I said with a wicked grin of my own. "I fucking love it." Then I slid farther down to cup her pussy, finding she was dripping for me. Unable to help myself, I plunged two fingers inside her, setting her off.

Her velvety soft walls clamped down around my digits as she threw her head back on a sharp cry of my name. Watching her come apart in my arms was one of the sexiest things I'd ever seen. I drove my fingers in and out of her, dragging out her release until her limbs gave out.

I kept her on her feet with an arm around her waist, my other hand still between her silky thighs. "Ah, ah, ah," I tsked, giving my head a shake. "I don't recall giving you permission to come."

She blinked, her eyes bleary as she struggled to clear her head after that release. "Sorry," she said on a breath before confessing, "It's been a while."

And damn if that didn't make me even harder for her. My cock was practically weeping with desperation.

"You don't ever have to apologize for that, my little Wildcat." A slow, languid smile tugged at her lips. "But as punishment, you're going to have to beg me for your next release."

Her tongue came out to sweep across her bottom lip. "Hunter?"

I traced its path with my thumb. "Yeah, Sere?"

"Please fuck me. I'm going to lose my mind if I don't feel you inside me."

She begged so fucking well, there was no way I could deny her. In seconds, we were both stripped completely bare. I flipped her around to face the island and pressed a hand between her shoulder blades until she was bent across the surface, all that long, sunshine hair spread out, her lush, tempting body spread out like my own personal feast.

I bent my knees, holding on to my cock as I guided it through her hot, wet slit. A hiss slithered between my teeth just as the crown notched into place at her opening. I could feel the heat coming from her core, and I wanted to drive in until she was all I could feel. But that was a decision she had to make for herself. I wasn't going to take it from her.

"I'm clean, baby," I said, feeling like I'd just run a goddamn marathon. "I just had my physical two months ago."

Pushing up onto her elbows, she twisted to look back at me over her shoulder, sending her hair sliding across her smooth, creamy skin. "I'm on the pill," she announced. "And I'm clean too."

I felt like my dick was about to explode. "Tell me I can

have you bare, Serenity. I need to feel every inch of you around me."

"Fuck me, Hunter." Her voice was liberally laced with desperation. "Please hurry."

With a snap of my hips, I drove myself into her, causing both of us to cry out. I couldn't remember ever feeling something as good as her pussy felt, squeezing me like a slick fist.

I could feel her pulsing around me and see the frantic rise and fall of her back as she fought for breath.

Skating a hand from her hip, up the ridge of her spine, to the back of her neck, I asked, "You okay?"

She cast a foggy smile over her shoulder. "So much better than okay, honey. Don't stop. I need you to make me come again."

She could take instruction brilliantly.

I shifted my hips, pulling nearly all the way out before slamming back in, again and again. With each thrust, she got wetter, making it easier for me to slide in as deep as I could possibly go.

The whole time I fucked her into the counter, she continued to beg, chanting my name and telling me how good my cock felt. A trail of sweat started at the base of my neck and slid down the center of my back as I pounded into her, her soft, supple flesh squeezing and clenching with each stroke.

It was, hands down, the best sex I'd ever had. And I hadn't even gotten off yet.

"Hunter," she gasped, bracing her palms on the thick

quartz countertop so she could push up and drive herself back into me with each forward snap of my hips. "I'm so close."

My spine started to tingle and my balls drew up tight to my body. "I'm right there with you, Wildcat. Let go and let me feel it."

Two strokes later, she clamped around my cock like a vise, throwing her head back as the most intoxicating sounds burst from her throat. A second later, I joined her in the abyss, pouring myself into her tight sheath as she milked me dry. By the time we both finished, we were gasping for breath as we collapsed across the island.

"Jesus," I grunted, pressing my forehead between her shoulder blades. "I'm not sure I can move."

Her tinkling giggle was like wind chimes. "If you do, I'm liable to melt right into the floor."

I trailed kisses along her back and neck before finding the energy to stand upright, my dick still tucked inside her. Only then did I remember the delicious dinner she'd prepared for me.

"You think the lasagna's still hot?"

Her shoulders shook on a laugh. "Yeah, honey. But if not, it'll microwave easy enough and still taste incredible."

TWENTY-THREE

SERENITY

Turned, out the lasagna was still warm enough we didn't need to nuke it.

After the workout we'd just had, both of us were starving, so we got dressed, Hunter in only his jeans, the zipper done, but the button still hanging open, and me in my panties and the tee Hunter had been wearing before fucking me damn near through the island.

We ate and talked and laughed, and Hunter surprised the hell out of me by revealing he was actually pretty damn tactile once the dam had burst. For starters, he'd pulled my barstool so close to his, I was practically on top of him. Then, between bites of food, he caresses my bare leg or reaches up to sift his fingers through my hair like he couldn't get enough.

"Damn, Wildcat," he groaned around the heaping bite he'd just taken. "This is the best lasagna I've ever tasted."

Heat hit my cheeks and I knew they'd flushed red at

the compliment. "Thanks," I said softly, a pleased smile taking over my face. "I love cooking and haven't done it in a while. It was nice to get to flex that muscle again."

He swallowed and wiped his mouth with a napkin before leaning in, taking my chin in his hand, and tilting my face up to his. He brushed a slow, sensuous, feather-light kiss against my lips. "If all your cooking tastes this damn good, I'm more than happy to let you flex that muscle in my kitchen as long as you want."

I'd been so sure I'd made too much, but when I looked back at the pan, I noticed Hunter had made more than a serious dent with the seconds and thirds he'd loaded on his plate.

"I don't know," I said playfully as I raked my gaze down his chest and abs. God, I could look at him all damn day. "You keep eating this much, you might get a bit of a gut, and I'm using you for your body, so you'll have to be sure to get some extra workouts in."

He lowered the fork that had been halfway to his mouth, slowly turning his head to look at me.

"Is that so?" he asked, his menacing tone and a look that promised payback sending a pleasurable shiver down my spine.

I nodded, biting my cheek to keep from laughing.

The static in the air snapped a moment later, and I bolted off my stool just as Hunter's fork clattered to the counter.

A peal of laughter bubbled past my lips as I ran past the living room, but I didn't even make it to the hall before he caught me. With a show of strength that sent a zap from my nipples to my clit, Hunter threw me over his shoulder and started for his bedroom.

"I'll show you who needs extra workouts," he growled, bringing his palm down against my ass in a stinging slap, making me yelp and my insides quiver.

Then he threw me onto his mattress and proceeded to give me the workout of my life.

———

I couldn't remember the last time I'd been so comfortable.

After round two, Hunter had ordered me to stay in bed while he headed back into the kitchen. I'd been floating on a cloud of bliss and orgasms as I listened to the sounds of him cleaning the kitchen. Knowing he was that kind of man, the kind to take care to clean the kitchen his woman had cooked in for him, had me losing a tiny piece of my heart.

I'd nearly dozed off when he returned a few minutes later, with two bowls piled high with ice cream sundaes.

"You took care of dinner, I figured I'd handle dessert. It's not a culinary masterpiece or anything like you'd probably bake, but I did the best with what I had."

With that show of sweetness, Hunter claimed another little piece of my heart. I took the bowl and held it out so I could lean in and kiss him, nice and deep.

"Ice cream sundaes are perfect," I whispered once I pulled back.

Silence engulfed the room as we sat snuggled in Hunter's bed, eating dessert, and I was finally able to wrap my head around everything that had happened the past few hours.

Questions floated through my mind on an endless loop, and he must have read them on my face, because before I was halfway into my sundae, he took the bowl from my hand and placed it on the nightstand beside his.

"I wasn't done with that," I decreed, but he didn't seem to care because he came back to me and used his body to guide me onto my back so he could hover over me.

"Hunter, as thrilling as the last few hours have been, I need a bit of a break. You're bigger than I'm used to, and I'm feeling it."

The smirk he gave me was full of arrogance. He lowered himself down to give me a kiss before pushing back up so he could see my face.

"As much as I like hearing that, and as much as I want you again, that's not what this is.

I widened my eyes as I lifted my arms and looped them around his neck. "Color me curious, then. What exactly is this?"

Those glacial eyes looked warm for the first time since I'd known him as he scanned my face, and the sight of his shadowless blue eyes was enough to steal my breath.

"I saw those wheels turning in that head of yours. They were spinning so fast I could hear them. This position is two-fold. It's my way of getting and keeping your attention so you can tell me what's on your mind, but it's also my way of maintaining contact, because now that I've touched you, I can't seem to stop."

Damn it, he had to be too good to be true. I was having a lot of trouble reconciling the man currently pinning me to his mattress with the one who, weeks ago, had told me the kiss we'd shared was a mistake.

"That right there," I started. "It's comments like that that had the wheels in my head spinning. You said nothing would ever happen between us. I tried to respect that, really. But it feels like everything you've done since that proclamation has been what a man does when he's pursuing a woman. It's been confusing as hell."

His brow furrowed as contrition stole across his features. "I know, baby." He leaned in, brushing his nose against mine. "And I'm sorry for that."

I appreciated that, but it wasn't really the answer I was looking for. "I hate being this woman, Hunter, but I feel like I have to ask: What are we doing here?"

There were so many conflicting emotions in his eyes, it tore at my chest.

"If this was only a one-time thing, say it. I'm a big girl. I can handle it." It would hurt like hell, but I'd force myself to get through. "I need to know where I stand. I'm not asking for a ring or a commitment you don't have in you to give. I just want the truth."

I could see the war waging inside of him through his eyes. He inhaled so deeply I worried he might burst a lung. "The truth is, I don't know."

Well that fucking stung. Suddenly, our position on his

bed lost its appeal. I knew I said I was a big girl, and I could handle it, but *shit*, that hurt.

I tried my best not to let it show, blinking rapidly and breathing deep to keep the tears at bay. I'd gotten damn good at hiding my emotions in my old life, and I pulled that little skill back out because I didn't want Hunter to see.

When I finally felt like I could speak past the lump in my throat, I nodded. "Well, okay, then."

I was expecting him to move, to free me from the bed so I could get up and make some excuse to be *anywhere* else, but he didn't. He continued to speak.

"I'm not someone you want to tie yourself to, Sere. I've got so much damage, it wouldn't be fair to ask you to take that on. But I'd be lying if I said I wasn't drawn to you from the moment I first laid eyes on you."

Well, I certainly hadn't been expecting *that*.

But he wasn't finished.

"I remember everything from that moment. Storming that warehouse to save you and your sister, only to find you whaling on the asshole who took you, dressed to fucking kill for the date you'd been on before being kidnapped. I felt an instant pang of jealousy for a man I'd never seen in my life."

Until that moment, I'd forgotten all about that date. But I was glad to know the dress had been a hit, at least.

"I want you in a way I can't explain. It doesn't make any sense, and now that I've had you, sorry to say it, baby, but I'm addicted."

"Hunter—"

"I know it's not fair to ask you this, but can you give me a day at a time? I don't know where this is going or how long it'll last before I fuck it up, but I've felt better with you in my life these past couple months than I've ever felt before. Baby, you keep the nightmares away. I didn't think that was possible."

"Nightmares?"

He let out an exhale that sounded like it carried the weight of the world. "Just a part of that damage I mentioned earlier. I've got more scars than the ones you can see on the outside."

I licked my lips, hesitating before finding the nerve to ask, "From the bombing?"

"Among other things."

God, what else could have happened to this poor man that rivaled something like that?

"Honey, I'm trying to be cool right now, I swear, but when you say things like that, it's almost impossible not to get curious."

He let out a weary sigh before moving his weight off me, shifting us both in the bed so his back was pressed up against the headboard and I was straddling his thighs.

He rested his hands on my hips, and I got the sense he was bracing for a story, so I kept my mouth shut and waited, determined to give him all the time he needed.

"Not a lot of people know this, but I had a little sister."

The use of past tense in that sentence made my skin

prickle, and all of a sudden I regretted my decision to push. "Hunter, you don't have to—"

He cut me off, his eyes growing unfocused as he returned to the memory. "Her name was Gracie. I was already fourteen by the time she was born, and back then, I thought the knowledge that my folks still had sex was the most damaging thing in the world. My parents liked the joke that she was a happy accident they had late in life. I didn't want a little sister at first, but the minute she was born, she had me wrapped around her little finger.

I bit the inside of my cheek to keep from crying at the wistfulness in his voice as he spoke of his baby sister.

"She was the light of my life," he continued, each word driving a knife a little deeper into my heart. "But I was still a stupid kid. I was dating this girl, Cindy Mitchell, and I snuck out one night to go fool around with her in the back of her parents' car. I was seventeen years old, thinking with my dick, and my whole life went up in flames at night. Literally."

I inhaled deeply, feeling a pain in my lungs and chest. "Honey, I shouldn't have pushed. I'm sorry. You really don't have to do this."

He shook his head, a sad smile pulling out his lips. "It's okay. She deserves to be talked about. She deserves to be remembered. I got home that night, and the fire was already so big I couldn't get close to the house. It was coming through the roof and windows. Investigators said it was a faulty water heater. My parents had just had a new one installed, and apparently the guy didn't know shit about putting in water heaters. It had been burning for a while by the time I got home. My parents died in their beds, smoking inhalation. Apparently, that's one of the better ways to go, but I don't know." He shook his head, grief etched into every line of his face.

"In my dreams I still hear Gracie's voice calling for me, begging me to help, to save her. I tried; I just couldn't do it."

"Hunter, it's not your fault. It was just an accident."

"The flames were so high, so hot, it felt like they were melting my skin when I got closer, but I couldn't leave her. I had to try. I rushed inside, and the smoke was so thick it started choking me instantly. I screamed for her, but she didn't respond. By the time I found her it was too late. I didn't know that at the time, one of the paramedics told me afterward. I was trying to rush out of the house, carrying a little body in my arms, when one of the ceiling joists gave away and fell on me."

"That's where the scars on your back came from," I said, in a barely-there whisper. He nodded. "I thought they were from the bombing."

His hands clenched on my hips, his fingers digging into my flesh. "Like I said, I've got scars inside and out. More than my fair share. If I wasn't dreaming about Gracie, screaming for me to help her, it was that boy with the goddamn rocket launcher. I haven't had a break from those nightmares in years."

He blinked, his eyes suddenly going clear as he shook himself from the past and looked at me.

"Until you. Granted, that couch is as uncomfortable as shit, but at least it hasn't been the nightmares waking me up."

He was trying to make light of the situation now that he'd poured all the heavy out, but I couldn't bring myself to follow his lead. Reaching up, I took his face in my hands and tilted it until his gaze locked with mine. After everything he'd just given me, after all the pain and suffering he'd endured in his life, the very least I could do was give him what he asked for. "I can give you one day at a time."

His shoulders sagged in relief, the tension melting from his bones like ice on a hot sidewalk in the middle of summer. "I don't want to make you any promises I'm not sure I can keep. But I'll do my best to make it worth it."

I didn't bother telling him he already had; he was worth this small sacrifice and so much more, because something in my gut told me he wouldn't believe me.

He wasn't ready to hear that yet, but I made a promise right then and there that I'd eventually get him there.

And one day, he'd know he was worth *everything*.

TWENTY-FOUR
SERENITY

The past week and a half had been some of the best days of my life.

I'd finally been able to go back to work a few days ago and was relieved to know that Fletcher was still in the dark about everything that had happened. He thought I'd been out with a nasty stomach flu, and when I finally got back, he'd actually been happy to see me. Sure, he hadn't been overly emotional about it, but he *had* said he was glad to see me, and the look on his face told me he meant it.

I was still crashing at Hunter's place but gone were the nights of him sleeping on the couch. Now he slept in bed next to me every night, holding me close, almost as though he was scared I'd slip away in his sleep.

Things between us were going better than I could have expected, and with each passing day, I fell harder and harder for him.

On the evenings I wasn't at the bar, I made him dinner, and he made sure to let me know with his actions and words just how much he appreciated my effort. It was nice having someone to cook for, and he was always so complimentary of everything I made, eating so much there were never any leftovers.

On the nights I worked, he came into the bar and took up residence on a barstool, drinking a couple beers or simply hanging out and chatting with me whenever I had a free moment. Then he'd take me home and rub my tired feet.

He was the perfect man. Or at least the perfect man for me.

We made love every single night, and some mornings he woke me up, needing me in a way that felt almost desperate. I had to say, that feeling was a high I'd never experienced before.

When we weren't together, we texted constantly, and with every day that passed, I was falling deeper and deeper for the man.

It was finally the weekend of the wedding, and while I was excited, looking forward to a big party and getting to spend some time with Bryce and Tessa, Hunter had been tenser than usual.

I chocked it up to it being the widow of a close friend he'd lost, but he'd been pretty tight-lipped about the whole thing. In an attempt to get him in the spirit of the weekend, I'd downloaded a ton of awesome songs for the road trip to Charlotte and bought key road-trip snacks for us to munch on.

The weather was perfect, so I'd rolled down my window, cranked the radio up, and belted out the lyrics to some of my favorite songs until I finally got him to smile. He'd refused to sing along with me but seemed more than happy to listen to me.

The hotel where the wedding and reception were being held had taken my breath away when we'd first pulled up the day before the big event. I'd wanted to go exploring but one second after the door to our room clicked shut behind us, Hunter was on me like a man stranded in the middle of the desert, and I was a glass of water.

We'd torn at each other's clothes and fucked so hard and hungrily that I was sure the people in the room beside us had been able to hear. When I woke up in the morning, I could still feel the twinge between my thighs.

As much as I loved spending time with him, I'd been grateful for the reprieve that morning when he left to have breakfast with Vera's sons.

With time to kill, I'd called Tessa, and together, we'd headed for the hotel spa for a little pampering.

We were sitting side by side in massage chairs with our feet soaking in warm water full of essential oils while nail techs gave us luxurious manicures when Tessa asked, "So how are things going with you and Hunter?"

I peeled my eyes open, ultimate relaxation plus a night of energetic sex making me feel a little drowsy. "Depends.

Are you asking out of curiosity, or because you've got money in the pool?"

She let out a sweet giggle and shook her head, her shiny light brown hair swishing across her shoulders. She was a serious stunner, no doubt about it, and sweet as hell. I was really glad we'd had this time to get to know each other better. "No, I decided not to bet on this one since I kept losing money. But I'm pretty sure Bryce put a hundred in."

I dropped my head back on a groan.

"But don't worry about it," she insisted. "If he loses, that's his own damn fault. I'm not going to ask you to sway things his way."

I smiled and relaxed back into the massage chair, letting the rolling wheels work my muscles. I'd been getting a hell of a workout lately, and my poor body was starting to pay for it.

"Things are going good," I admitted giddily. "Really good. We're taking things a day at a time right now, but I'm happy."

"Ah, I love that. You deserve it. And so does he."

"You've known him for a long time, right? Like, from before . . ."

She smiled, but there was a sadness behind her eyes. "Not well. Bryce and I met during a whirlwind weekend in Vegas. He was there with Hunter, and two more members of their team."

"Moss and Danielson?"

Her eyes widened in surprise. "He told you about them?"

"A little. I know he and Bryce lost them both in the same bombing Hunter lost his leg in. It was obvious he cared deeply about both of them and he's still hurting over their loss."

She nodded, her eyes going glassy with tears she was desperately trying to fight back. "Losing them changed both Bryce and Hunter. They have so much guilt for being the ones to come back when their brothers weren't as lucky. That's why Bryce and I were apart for so long. He was punishing himself, carrying the blame because he was the lead on that mission. He convinced himself he didn't deserve happiness, so when they got back, he disappeared and it broke my heart."

I reached across the distance between us and took the hand that wasn't currently being buffed and polished. "I'm sorry," I said gently, hating that a woman as kindhearted and good as Tessa had suffered so much while she and Bryce had been apart.

It had been sheer coincidence that brought her to Hope Valley. She'd come for a job interview as the director of Hope House, and the rest, as they say, was history. Their romance had been rekindled instantly, at least on Bryce's part. He'd pulled out all the stops in order to win her back, and luckily he'd succeeded. Now they were living their happily ever after, and had their first baby a few months ago.

"It was hard," she admitted, "but looking back on it now, I can't say I would change anything. Bryce needed to work through what happened in that desert on his own. If he'd come back to me right away, I'm not sure we would have made it. When we ran into each other again, he was finally ready to battle his demons."

I felt that down to my bones. Hunter had more demons than I would wish on my worst enemy, and he was still battling them to this day. I wanted to help him through, to take his hand and lead him from that darkness, but I wasn't sure it was my place. As quickly as I was falling for him, I still felt like there was a wall between us, and the only person who could scale it was Hunter.

"He's been anxious the past few days," I confessed, feeling a bit of the weight I'd been carrying fall away at having someone to talk to about everything. Someone who understood everything I was up against. "There's like, this restless energy building in him, ready to explode. Maybe because it's Moss's widow, it's dredging up a lot of things from his past, but he won't talk about it."

"That might very well be the case. All I know for sure is, he's been happier lately than I've seen him in years. Whatever you're doing, keep doing it, because he deserves someone as amazing as you. Just be patient with him. If there's anything I've learned, it's that these guys have to fall down a bunch of times before they finally get things right."

I could do that, I could hang in there because I already knew Hunter was worth it.

By the time I got back to the room, Hunter was already back. He was stretched out across the bed, his back resting against the headboard, ankles crossed as he flipped through the channels on the television.

"Hey, how was your breakfast?" I asked as I tossed my room key onto the dresser and moved across the room to him.

He tossed the remote aside as soon as I was close enough and reached out to tag my arm and yanked me down into his lap.

"It was great," he said with a genuine grin, the tension that had been locking his muscles up for days now drifting away as the thought of those two boys. "I told them all about you. They're really excited to meet you."

"Aw," I leaned in to press my lips against his. "You told them about me? Swoon!" I might have been teasing, but it made me feel like a million bucks to hear I warranted mention to the boys he thought of as sons.

"Of course, I did," he stated simply.

I traced his smile, feeling my own lips tip upward. "I'm glad you had a good time. You really care about them, huh?"

He dragged his hand up and down my spine, his touch so tender it made me misty-eyed. "Love them like they're mine. Miss them every damn day too. But Luke talked about looking at colleges in Virginia when the time comes."

I could tell by the tone of his voice that he loved the idea of one of his boys being closer, and that warmed something deep inside of me. If it made him happy, I wanted it for him. "That's exciting. I hope that works out so you can have him closer."

A smirk curled the corners of his mouth upward. "Speaking of getting closer," he rasped as he tightened his grip on my waist, making me laugh.

"Not a chance, stud. I need to hop in the shower or we're going to be late."

A delectable hum rattled up his throat. "It just so happens I do some of my best work in the shower."

My head tipped back on a deep belly laugh. I loved this playful side of him. "Believe me, I'm well aware, but I'm going to have to pass. We start that up, we'll never make it downstairs."

"Works for me," he grunted, and I had the distinct impression that he meant it.

"Yeah, well, you promised me a party, so I'm going to hold you to it." As hard as it was, I climbed off his lap and out of the bed. "But I promise I'll make it up to you later tonight," I said, bending forward to place a kiss against his lips before starting for the bathroom.

"I'm gonna hold you to that," he called after me, making me smile.

———

I'd just pulled my dress out of the closet and laid it across the bed when a knock sounded on the door.

Cinching the hotel robe I was wearing tighter, I padded across the room and threw the door open. A woman I'd never seen before stood on the other side, her mouth poised to speak, but the moment her eye landed on me, they widened, like I was a shock to her.

Her hair was twisted and curled into an intricate updo, and her makeup was obviously professionally done, a juxtaposition to the yoga pants and T-shirt she was wearing.

"Hi," I greeted, tilting my head to the side. "Can I help you?"

"Oh, uh—no. I don't—" Her gaze darted around like she was searching for something. "Sorry. I didn't mean to bother you. I think I might have the wrong room."

"Oh, okay. Well, who are you looking for? I'm not sure I'll be much help, but you're welcome to come in and use our phone to call the front desk."

"I was looking for Hunter McCann," she said. "My son gave me this room number."

"You're in the right place," I announced, a strange sensation crawling over my skin at her answer. "But he's in the shower right now."

"Oh." She blinked, her eyes going wide. "*Oh*. You—you're his date. He brought a date," she said, like the thought shocked the living hell out of her.

"Yeah. I'm Serenity." I offered my hand to her. "It's nice to meet you . . ." I left the end of my sentence hanging, giving her a chance to provide her name.

"Vera," she replied, taking my hand and giving it a weak shake.

"The bride!" I chirped, the puzzle pieces of her appearance at our door suddenly falling into place. "Of course! It's so nice to meet you. Hunter's told me all about you."

She was still holding my hand, slowly lifting it up and down. "He has?" she asked in bewilderment.

I didn't understand the question, and if I were being honest, this whole exchange seemed weird. Her hair and makeup made sense now that I knew who she was, but I was surprised she'd taken the time to come up to our room when she should have been getting ready for *her wedding*. It didn't make sense to me. "Of course. Would you like to come in? He should be out soon. We're just getting ready for—well, your wedding," I finished with an awkward laugh.

"No, no. That's okay. I just thought I'd swing by and say hello. It's been a while since we've seen each other." She gave her head a shake. "I'm sorry. I didn't know he brought a date, or I wouldn't have—you know what? Never mind. It doesn't matter. I should get back downstairs. I'll see you guys at the wedding."

Before I could get another word in, she whipped around on her flip-flops and darted down the hall toward the elevator leaving me with a strange, unexplainable feeling in the pit of my stomach.

TWENTY-FIVE

SERENITY

Something had changed the moment I told Hunter about Vera showing up at our hotel room door. He carried himself like his muscles were straining and the energy pouring off him was like static electricity crackling in the air.

He'd gone silent as we finished getting ready, not speaking a word until I stepped out of the bathroom, dress on, hair in place, and makeup perfected.

"Damn," he said on a breath, his eyes going hot as he took me in. "Sere, baby, you take my breath away."

I moved into him, unable to help myself. He looked so damn delectable dressed in all black. The slacks and jacket looked like they were tailor-made for his impeccable body, and in typical Hunter fashion, he'd foregone a tie, choosing instead to keep the button at the collar of his black dress shirt undone.

A part of me wanted to say to hell with the wedding,

and climb him like a tree. But another part of me wanted to show him off. I was proud to be on his arm tonight, and I wanted the world to see that I'd landed my dream guy.

"What do you say? You ready to roll?"

And just like that, those storm clouds came rushing back in, hovering over him. I didn't understand what was going on or why his mood was flip-flopping so damn fast. I asked him on the elevator ride down to the ballroom if something was wrong, but all he did was take my hand and give me a wan smile before insisting, "Everything's great, Wildcat. Just not a huge fan of weddings."

Tessa and Bryce were waiting near the elevators when the doors opened in the lobby.

"Oh my God," Tessa exclaimed the moment she saw me. "Sere, you look beautiful."

I blushed at her compliment and scanned her up and down. "Right back at you, babe." I took her hands and leaned in, placing a kiss on her cheek. "That dress is something else."

Bryce pulled his wife flush against his side, his eyes brimming with heat and adoration as he gazed down at her. "My woman looks incredible in anything," he proclaimed proudly.

I felt a bit sentimental as I watched them together. They really did make a beautiful couple, and I was unbelievably happy both of them had been able to find their happy ending after so many years of sadness and pain.

I snapped out of my musings when Hunter's arm

came around me, gently pulling me against his strong, solid body so he could press his lips to my temple.

The tender action brought a smile to my face as I tipped my head up to look at him. The storm clouds were still there, but a bit of light shined through as he locked gazes with me.

"You good?" I asked quietly.

"I'm good, baby," he insisted before using his hold on me to turn us both, starting in the direction of the ballroom where the wedding ceremony was taking place. "Let's get this over with so I can get you back upstairs and strip you naked."

A shiver worked its way over my skin, and I had to clamp the inside of my cheek to keep from moaning. Now was so not the time.

We were greeted at the large, ornate double doors by two teenagers dressed in crisp, black tuxes. The moment we stepped into view, their faces broke into huge, shit-eating grins.

"Uncle Hunt!" the younger of the two exclaimed.

The switch in Hunter flipped again as he pulled me with him. "Liam. Lookin' sharp, kid." He reached out and ruffled the boy's hair, making his cheeks flush. The older boy came over to join his brother, and Hunter quickly made introductions. "Luke, Liam, this is my girl, Serenity." I melted a little at hearing *my girl*. "Sere, baby, these are my boys, Luke and Liam."

Both of them preened under Hunter's attention, and it was obvious how important they all were to each other.

After discovering all the loss Hunter had suffered in his life, it filled me with relief to know he at least had this.

"It's so good to meet you," I told them, smiling wide. "Hunter's spoken so highly of both of you, I've been looking forward to this."

Liam blushed even deeper and ducked his head while Luke shifted his cheeky grin to the man he called uncle and declared, "Well done, Uncle Hunt. She's a stunner."

Now it was my turn to blush as Hunter pulled me into his side. "Don't I know it, boy."

Luke's grin grew even wider.

"What am I, invisible?" Bryce declared from behind us.

The boys shifted their excitement from seeing Hunter to Bryce and greeted him and Tessa with the same level of enthusiasm. They chatted as long as they could before Luke announced, "We're pulling double duty as ushers before walking Mom down the aisle, so we better get you guys to your seats."

Without the distraction of the boys, Hunter grew stiff once more as we took our seats and waited for the ceremony to begin.

In an effort to distract him from whatever was messing with his head, I leaned in and whispered, "I can see why you love those boys so much. They're pretty incredible."

He gave me a soft look and linked his fingers with mine, lifting my hand to brush a kiss against my knuckles. "You're incredible."

God, he made it impossible not to love him.

I blinked, warmth blooming in my chest and spreading

far and wide. "You make me happy," I blurted, unable to stop the words from pouring out. "I need you to know that. One day at a time. But no matter what happens in the future, know that you made me happy."

He pulled in the deepest breath before squeezing his eyes closed and pressing his forehead against mine. "You undo me, sweetheart."

The music started and the moment was over as everyone turned to watch the wedding party start down the aisle.

———

Hunter

"You make me happy."

The words played over and over in my head on a steady loop as the bridesmaids made their way from the back of the ballroom to the altar at the front.

Vera's husband-to-be, Oliver, stood front and center, his throat bobbing on a thick swallow as he shifted from foot to foot anxiously. He was the complete antithesis to the kind of man Craig had been. It wasn't necessarily a fair comparison. After all, I didn't know this guy from Adam. The boys said he was nice and treated their mom like she walked on water, but he was the kind of dude who sat behind a desk all day long, crunching numbers and creating spreadsheets. He'd probably never experienced anything worse than a papercut, for Christ's sake.

As if reading my thoughts and agreeing completely, Bryce leaned in on my other side and asked under his breath, "That's the new guy?"

I grunted in the affirmative.

"Guy looks like a fuckin' shrimp."

Tessa hissed and shoved an elbow into her husband's ribs. "Be nice. He could be a very . . ." She struggled to find a compliment before finally settling on, "sweet man."

"Well, I sure the fuck hoped so, because I don't know what else the man could possibly have going for him," Bryce returned in a hushed voice.

In response, Serenity snorted, drawing my attention. She was desperately trying to suppress her laughter and hiding her hysterical grin behind her hand.

I hadn't been looking forward to this day one goddamn bit, but with her by my side, it suddenly felt so much easier.

Then again, most things seemed easier with her around.

The music swelled, the Wedding March picked up, and the doors opened, revealing the woman who had me tied in knots from the first moment I met her years and years ago, the only woman I'd convinced myself I'd ever love.

I hadn't seen her in so long, that first glance of her walking down the aisle in that glittering white dress was a blow to the gut. She was still as beautiful as I remembered, but there was something different about the feelings stirring inside me.

Memories of the past slammed into me like a wrecking ball, but my heart didn't clench and start to race like it used to, and I realized in that moment, I'd been putting the memory of Vera on a pedestal for so long, I hadn't allowed anything else to live up to it.

She smiled, that perfect, straight white smile that you'd expect to see in a toothpaste commercial as her eyes darted around the room.

She was only feet away from our aisle, when our eyes locked, and her smile faltered. Something shifted over her expression as she held my gaze captive. It looked a whole hell of a lot like melancholy, but before I could give it more thought, Serenity's delicate fingers squeezed my hand and pulled me back to the present, throwing my focus from Vera to her.

When I looked down, that bright, sunny smile I loved so damn much was gone. Her face was pulled into a frown, and I knew she had seen everything that had been coming off Vera and slamming into me.

I knew I'd fucked up royally, not controlling my reaction, when I tried to tighten my hold on her hand, but she pulled away, clasping her palms together and tucking them into her lap. She might not have known exactly what she just saw, hell, I wasn't certain myself, but she knew whatever it was, it wasn't something that should've happened as long as she was sitting by my side.

I spent the rest of the ceremony wracking my brain,

trying to figure out what the hell I was going to say to Serenity, how I was going to fix this.

And by the time the officiant pronounced Oliver and Vera husband and wife, and the crowd stood to applaud the happy couple, I wasn't any closer to a solution.

TWENTY-SIX
HUNTER

The second the last of the wedding party disappeared behind the double doors, we were shuffled toward the back of the room where the open bar had been set up so the space could be converted to the reception.

I couldn't get to that goddamn bar fast enough. I needed a drink almost as much as I needed my next breath.

I got a whiskey for me, needing more than a beer at the moment, and a glass of champagne for Serenity.

"Thanks," she said quietly as she wrapped her fingers around the long narrow flute and brought it to her lips, drinking down half in one go.

I wrapped my arm around her waist and held her close, bending my neck in an effort to meet her eyes, but she was going out of her way to look anywhere but at me. "You good?" I asked, feeling a sinking sensation deep in my stomach.

The smile she gave me wasn't nearly as bright and happy as the one I'd seen a million times. "Yeah. Great," she chirped, the lie ringing clear in her voice. "I need to use the restroom. Will you excuse me?"

I didn't want to let her go. I wanted to drag her back to our room and bury myself deep until neither one of us remembered anything outside of the way we made each other feel.

But I knew that wouldn't help anything.

"I'll go with you," Tessa announced, and I let out a sigh of relief that Serenity wouldn't be alone, even if only for a couple minutes.

I watched the woman who had clawed her way under my skin leave the ballroom, feeling as though she was taking a piece of me with her.

It wasn't until Bryce slugged me in my arm to get my attention that I was able to pull my focus from the last place I'd seen Serenity.

"Jesus," I grunted, rubbing my stinging arm. "What the fuck, asshole?"

"I should be asking *you* what the fuck," he clipped.

I downed my drink in a couple swallows and set the glass back on the bar before waving at the bartender for a refill. "I don't know what the hell you're talking about."

He reared back, his brows creeping high on his forehead. "Really? Then that would make you the only fucking one. Don't know if you can feel the eyes of every damn body in the room on you right now, but just in case you're blind, there wasn't a single person who missed the eye fucking the goddamn bride gave you on her way down the aisle to her *husband*."

Shit.

I dragged my gaze through the room, and sure enough, several people were staring in my direction, most of them whispering behind their hands, no doubt discussing what they'd witnessed.

"Fucking hell," I groaned, reaching up to drag my fingers through my hair. "Was it really that bad?"

He looked at me like I'd lost my mind. "You saw the look on Sere's face before she bolted to the bathroom, right? What the hell do you think?"

"She came to our room before the wedding," I confessed as I gulped my second drink, savoring the burn as it traveled down my throat and settled in my gut.

Bryce's jaw dropped. "Tell me you're joking."

I shook my head. "Not even a little."

"Of fucking course she did," he bit out coarsely. "What the hell did she want?"

I lifted my shoulder in a shrug. "No idea. I was in the shower. Sere answered it, said the interaction seemed strange."

"I'd say. The woman was supposed to be getting ready for one of the biggest days of her life, yet she still took the time to hunt you down. Who does that?"

"Ladies and gentlemen," the deejay announced over the speaker system, effectively cutting off anything else Bryce had to say. "Put your hands together for Mr. and Mrs. Oliver James!"

The crowd burst into applause as the doors swung open once more and the happy couple came sauntering through, hand in hand.

While everyone rushed to them, eager to give out well wishes and blessings on a happy union, Bryce and I remained at the bar, separated from the crowd.

The goddamn party Serenity had been looking forward to hadn't even started, and already, I wanted this goddamn night to be over.

From the corner of my eye, I saw a flash of white separate from the crowd and start in our direction.

"Aren't you two a sight for sore eyes," Vera exclaimed. She moved into Bryce and lifted up on her toes to place a kiss against his cheek. "It's so good to see you. Thank you for coming."

"Of course," he returned, the smile he was giving the happy bride nowhere near his eyes. "It's been a long time."

"It sure has been," she said with a sigh, shifting her attention to me as she added, "Way too long."

Fuck me.

She moved to me, giving me the same greeting she'd just given Bryce, only her kiss lingered on my cheek longer than necessary. "Congratulations," I said as I took a step back, putting some space between us. "You made a beautiful bride."

She looked up at me through her lashes, her voice coming out low and throaty as she said, "Thank you. You know, I was hoping to catch up with you earlier. I swung by your room and met your date."

I ignored the pain that flashed across her face.

"Yeah, Sere told me."

"Sere," she said on a breath, like the endearment I used hurt her somehow. "She's very pretty."

"She's sweet as hell too," Bryce threw in, tossing gasoline onto a fire. "She's good for our man, Hunter. Nice to see him settling down."

He was laying it on way too fucking thick. I wanted to knock his teeth down his throat to shut him up.

Vera's lips parted slightly. "Wow. That's—I didn't know you were seeing anyone. Let alone it was so serious."

My eyes trailed to the door Serenity had gone through minutes ago, and the feeling that rushed over me just then came out of nowhere.

I missed her. She'd been gone a handful of minutes and I *missed* her. I couldn't stop looking at that goddamn door, waiting for her to come back to me so I could wrap my arm around her and keep her close the rest of the night.

"It is serious," I confessed, not only to Vera, but to myself as well.

I was done denying the truth of what she meant to me. *You make me happy.*

And damn if she didn't do the same for me.

"She makes me happy."

Vera's face looked stricken, the color leaching from her skin beneath her makeup, and with the epiphany that came with realizing I wanted Serenity in my life for the long haul, came the clarity about the woman I'd held above all others for almost half my life.

Everything Bryce and I had fought about for years was true.

She had used me.

I spent way too many years refusing to love someone else because I was too busy chasing after a fantasy. Then, easy as could be, she hung me out to dry like it was nothing once she finally got her life back together.

I couldn't put the blame solely on her. After all, I was the one who let her do it. I made her to be something so much bigger than what she was, and then stupidly built my world around her.

Even after packing up my life and moving to Hope Valley, I still clung to the dream of what was never going to happen. I let her manipulate me, dangling me from her hook the whole goddamn time, only to cut me loose when something better came along.

"I hope your new man makes you happy, Vera," I said, finality in my words.

Her face crumpled, desperation leaching out "Hunter," she breathed, "do you think we could maybe talk in private later?"

And there it was. She was *still* doing it.

I knew then and there that the only reason she'd showed up at my hotel room earlier was because she'd gotten word—probably from one of her sons—that I was there with another woman. She lived her life content to have me on her back-burner, always waiting as a backup plan in case something went wrong, and she was panicking at the realization she didn't have that anymore.

"That's not going to happen, Vera."

"But—"

"I'm in love with her." Christ, but that felt good to say. "You've moved on with your life. It's time to let me do the same."

With that, I turned and set my half-full drink down and went in search of the woman who reminded me what it was like to feel happiness.

As soon as I pushed through the door and out of the ballroom, I saw Tessa heading in my direction. Alone.

She stopped and stared at me, her expression conveying just how disappointed in me she was. Before I could get a word out, she held up her hand. "Before I tell you where she is, I have one thing to say." She paused to pull in a breath, like she was gearing up to rip into me. "I've known you a long time, Hunter. You're my family as much as you are Bryce's, and I've never seen you as settled as you are with Serenity. She gives you peace, and after everything you've been through, you deserve that. Don't screw this up."

For the millionth time I thought of how grateful I was that my brother lucked out and landed himself such an incredible woman. "I don't intend to," I assured her. "Now, where is she?"

"She went back to your room. Said she had a headache."

Shit.

I started for the elevators, only to have Tessa's voice

stop me. "You know, if it makes any difference, I love that woman. We all do."

It made all the difference in the world, because the people in Hope Valley were my family.

I smiled and tilted my chin in acknowledgment of what she'd just said, then I spun on my heel and rushed to the elevator, desperate to get to my woman.

———

Serenity

It all made perfect sense now; the strange encounter with the bride-to-be earlier that day, the way Hunter's mood seemed to flip back and forth, how tense he'd been the past few days leading up to the wedding.

The questions that had been bouncing around in my head, driving me crazy, for days, finally had answers, and they were answers that made me sick to my stomach.

I'd escaped to the bathroom for a small reprieve, but with Tessa's constant look of concern over the stares I got, that other wedding-goers had witnessed the same thing I had—the longing in the bride's eyes for a man who *wasn't* her betrothed; it had all become too much.

There was no way in hell I could go back into that ballroom and pretend everything was all sunshine and rainbows, so I'd made a lame excuse about having a headache that Tessa saw right through, and bolted for the sanctuary of my hotel room.

I would have given anything to be back in Hope Valley, somewhere that felt comfortable and safe, but I was stuck here for one more night.

As soon as I got to the room, I stripped off the dress I'd spent two days trying to find in order to impress a man who'd been in love with someone else this whole damn time.

God, I was such a freaking idiot.

I turned the shower to hot and climbed in, standing under the steady spray until my fingers turned pruney, then I scrubbed the makeup from my face and washed my hair clean of all the product I'd used to make it look nice.

The bathroom was full of steam and the mirror fogged over, by the time I climbed out and toweled off. I twisted my wet hair into another bun and wrapped the lush hotel robe around me before opening the door.

And as soon as I stepped out into the bedroom, the sight of Hunter sitting at the foot of the bed gave me a start.

He'd lost the jacket at some point, rolling up the sleeves of his button-down and showcasing those arms I loved so damn much.

"W-what are you doing here?" I stuttered, clutching the towel tighter.

"Waiting for you," he stated plainly. "Two more minutes and I would've busted into that bathroom to get to you."

I tried not to let his comment affect me, suppressing the shiver that skated down my back, but it was pointless. I was so gone for this man, there was no bother trying to deny it. Instead, I let out a sad sigh, and moved to where he sat, collapsing down on the mattress beside him.

"You're in love with her, aren't you?" I asked. It was a question I didn't want the answer to but needed all the same. I stared straight ahead as I waited for him to answer, unable to look at him. Finally, he spoke.

"I was. Once. Or at least I had convinced myself I was." That confounding statement was enough to yank my attention in his direction.

"What does that mean?"

"It means I've spent nearly half my life thinking I was in love with a woman I could never have. But then I met you, and I'm starting to think it was all a figment of my imagination." He turned those glacier eyes on me, and there wasn't a single storm cloud or shadow in sight. "Because what I feel for you is unlike anything I've ever experienced before."

My lungs seized and my heart begin to beat staccato against my ribs, pounding so hard it was a wonder it didn't sound like thunder crashing in our room.

"What are you saying?"

He shifted on the mattress, turning to face me fully, and reached out to cup my cheek in his large, strong hand. "I think you know what I'm saying, but if you need me to spell it out, I'm more than happy to do that. I'm in love with you, Serenity. You told me earlier that I make you happy, and what I failed to tell you at the time, but should have, was that you make me happy too. I haven't felt that in so long, I nearly forgot what it was like. Then you crashed into my life and lit it up with your sunshine. I thought I didn't deserve you. I've carried around so much guilt for so long. Guilt over not being there for my sister and parents, for not being able to save my team. I felt like I let everyone in my life down, and I couldn't stand the thought of letting you down too."

God, he was killing me. "Hunter, none of that was your fault. You didn't let anyone down. You see the scars on your body as damage, but that's not what they are." I couldn't sit there for another second and not touch him.

Reaching out, I placed my palms on the sides of his neck and slid my fingers into the short hair at the nape of his neck. "I see the scars on your body as a map of every-thing you went through, everything you endured in an effort to save those you cared about."

"Christ," he grunted, squeezing his eyes closed and pressing deeper into my touch. "I don't think anyone has ever seen me the way you do."

"That's their loss," I said in a barely-there voice. "Because you're the best man I've ever met, and I'm grateful each and every day that I get to have you in my life." I smiled then, a teasing smile that stretched my cheeks wide. "Even when we were pretending like we could only be friends."

I let out a yelp when he grabbed hold of my waist and tossed me onto the bed like I was as light as air. "I don't want you to go back to your apartment," he said once he was hovering over me, the weight of his strong body pressing me into the mattress and making me hot everywhere. "And not just because Cyrus is still out there. I don't want you to go back because I can't stand the thought of coming home from work every day and your face not being the first thing I see."

I pulled in a sharp breath as his beautiful words washed through me.

"You chased the nightmares away, Wildcat."

It took a great deal of effort, but I managed not to burst into ugly, happy sobs. "Then I guess I better stick around to make sure they don't come back," I said on a sniffle.

At my response, the smile he gave me was so gorgeous it stole the air from my lungs.

"I swear to you, I'll make your sacrifice worth it."

I laughed and wrapped my arms around him. "Oh, I have no doubt about that."

TWENTY-SEVEN
SERENITY

I ground down on Hunter's cock as he snapped his hips up, filling me deeper than any man ever had.

The pressure in my core grew more intense as I bit down on my lip with a whimper. "Baby, please," I begged, feeling like I was losing my mind. "I need to come. Please make me come."

"Goddamn," he grunted, shooting up to sit beneath me. One hand wrapped around me and fisted in my hair as the other lifted my breast to his mouth. He raked his teeth across my sensitive nipple before sucking it between his lips and pulling so deep I felt it in my clit, he released it with a loud pop, the grin he gave me downright wolfish. "My good girl knows how to beg the way I like it."

"Oh God," I cried as I continued to ride him, harder, faster, each roll of my hips becoming jerky and uncoordinated as my orgasm came barreling at me. "I can't hold back, Hunter."

"Let go," he ordered. "Come on my cock and milk me dry."

That was all it took. My release slammed into me like a freight train, my walls clamping down and the muscles in my body stringing tight as wave after wave pulled me under.

Hunter went over the edge a second later, grabbing my hips and slamming me down on him so he could empty himself inside me.

I would never get used to how good he made me feel, how every touch made me crave more.

It had been two weeks since the wedding, and if I thought things couldn't have been better before, I had been wrong, because without those shadows lingering and his past floating beneath the surface, everything between us was damn near perfect.

I'd gone from happy to blissful, and every day it kept getting better.

Using his hold on my hair, Hunter tilted my head down to his and kissed me, hot and hungry. "My Wildcat," he breathed, his voice filled with awe. "You have no idea how much I love you."

"Oh, I think I might have some idea," I said with a beaming grin. "After all, I started falling for you after that first kiss in the parking lot of the Tap Room months ago."

He shook his head. "Guess I'm just slow on the uptake."

I shrugged and dragged my fingers through his hair, loving that I could touch him whenever and wherever I wanted, as often as I wanted, because this amazing man was *all mine.*

"You caught on fast enough; consider yourself forgiven."

He hummed and went in for another kiss. "Call in sick, today," he spoke against my lips. "I'll do the same and we can spend the whole fucking day in bed."

"Tempting, but I can't. Sorry," I said, placing one last kiss on his lips before climbing from the bed and heading to the bathroom to clean up.

His pitiful groan followed after me. "You're killing me!"

"Then you'll have died a very happy man," I shouted over the running water as I turned the shower on.

Truth was, despite how much I loved spending time with Hunter, I didn't *want* to call in sick.

Fletcher had just been accepted to a university a couple hours away, and to celebrate his achievement, we were throwing him a little surprise party at the bar before his shift started. His whole Tap Room family would be there, as would the kids and volunteers from Hope House to take part in the celebration.

He's been so nervous when the letter arrived he hadn't been able to bring himself to open it. Instead, he held on to it until we had a shift together and brought it to the bar so I could read it first. I might have cried—more like sobbed—tears of joy when I finished the first sentence, congratulating him for getting in.

I was so damn proud of the kid for pushing past everything he'd suffered through, busting his ass to make himself a better life. He was strong enough not to let his past define him, to pick himself up and prove he could do better.

I was going to miss him desperately, but he'd promised to stay in touch, and I had every intention of holding him to that.

Thanks to Hunter's sadistic habit of holding me at the brink of orgasm for what felt like an eternity, making me beg before finally letting me plummet over, I was cutting it dangerously close to being late.

He was in the kitchen, fully dressed and drinking a cup of coffee by the time I came skidding down the hall, announcing, "We have to go, or I'm going to be late!"

He held up his keys to show he was ready and waiting. With Cyrus still in the wind, Hunter was still leery about letting me go off on my own, so he usually insisted on taking me in to work. If he couldn't do it, I had one of the other Alpha Omega badasses carting me around.

It had been nice at first, having my very own hot chauffeurs, but I was ready for this whole thing to be over so Hunter and I could get on with our lives. I felt like we were in some sort of holding pattern that wouldn't end until Cyrus was behind bars and the threat of him was no longer hanging over our heads.

"Just waiting on you, sweetheart."

I cut my eyes at him as I looped the strap of my purse over my shoulder. "Don't look so smug. It's your fault I'm almost late."

He didn't look the slightest bit repentant as he came over to me, giving me a loud, smacking kiss and slapping my ass. "Worth every fucking minute, baby. I will never get enough of you."

The feeling was entirely mutual.

By the time he pulled into the parking lot of the Tap Room, I was downright giddy, ready to surprise Fletcher, and show him just how many people cared about him.

"Have a good day," Hunter said before hooking me around the back of the neck and pulling me across the center console for a kiss. "Tell the kid I'm proud of him and he's gonna do great."

I smiled softly at my man, happiness radiating from my pores. "I will, honey. Love you."

"Love you more and forever." He'd started saying that the day after the wedding, and I would *never* get sick of hearing it.

With one last kiss, I climbed out of the car and headed for the bar, feeling like I was walking on a cloud. I had no idea that my own happy ending was going to be threatened by a deranged psychopath.

———

Fletcher

I woke up this morning with a pit in my stomach, a sense of dread clinging to me like a plastic bag stuck to a car antenna as it sped down the highway. Something bad was going to happen today. I'd tried to shake the sensation, but it wouldn't let go.

This was supposed to be a good day.

Ms. Serenity thought she'd been so clever, planning a surprise party for me because I got into college, but she was terrible at keeping secrets. More than once, I'd walked around a corner to find her standing with someone, discussing it at a loud enough volume I'd been able to hear her all the way down the hall. She'd been so excited that I couldn't bring myself to tell her I knew.

I didn't want to burst her bubble. And besides, it was kind of nice having someone care about me so damn much. I wasn't used to it, that was for sure. A lifetime with my father had taught me to expect the worst from people, but Ms. Serenity had been determined to prove that wrong.

Truthfully, I was sad to be leaving the Tap Room gang behind, but most especially her. She'd insisted we were a family, and the way she said it made me think she really believed it. I was going to miss her like crazy. I was going to miss all of them. But I'd come back. Once I made some-thing of myself and could show everyone how successful I was, I'd come back. And I'd repay Ms. Serenity for all the kindness she'd given me these past months ten-fold.

On that thought, I peddled my bike faster, as the Tap Room came into view. I'd just rounded the corner of the bar into the back alley where I kept it locked when the door by the dumpster swung open and Ms. Serenity came out, carrying a bag of trash.

I called her name and raised my arm to wave, but froze when a figure ducked out of the shadows right behind her. It was someone I'd recognize anywhere. The devil himself, made human.

"Ms. Serenity!" I shouted frantically.

She looked up at me and waved, that beautiful smile of hers stretched across her face so big you could see it from a mile away.

My blood turned to ice as I began peddling faster, like my life—or hers—depended on it. "Run!" I screamed, but it was too late.

My father lifted his arm, something I couldn't make out in his hand, and brought it down fast, slamming the object into her head so hard her whole body dropped like a lead balloon.

He scooped her up before she could hit the ground, and threw her over his shoulder, casting one last glance in my direction as I screamed for help and peddled so fast my heart felt like it was going to burst.

With a sick grin I'd seen too many times to count, he threw her limp body into the passenger side of his truck, raced around the hood, and slammed the driver side door. Then he peeled out of the alley.

I jumped off my bike without bringing it to a full stop and raced through the back door, running so fast my feet skidded across the floor once I reached the front of the bar.

"Whoa, kiddo," Ms. Rory laughed. "Slow down or you're liable to hurt yourself."

"Ms. Serenity," I panted, my lungs feeling like they would explode.

Reading the terror on my face, the humor fled from Ms. Rory's, and she rushed over to me, placing a comforting hand on my back as the rest of the people on shift gathered around me.

"What's wrong? What happened?"

"He took her," I wheezed.

The other bartender on duty, Dan, crouched to reach my eyes. "Who took her, kid?"

"My dad."

Everything that happened after that felt like it was going in slow motion and lightning speed all at the same time.

The bar burst into activity, because everyone knew what it meant. The devil having just stolen an angel, and we had to get her back.

Twenty-Eight

Serenity

I came to with a headache so bad it felt like a train was barreling through my skull. I cracked my eyes open, my vision blurry, and blinked against the harsh light shining in my eyes, making the pain even worse.

"What—what happened?" I moaned, my head feeling like it weighed a thousand pounds as I tried to lift it.

"About time you woke up," a voice that turned my blood to ice said. "Was afraid there for a while that I killed you before I got to have any fun."

Fear like I'd never experienced in my life crashed through me like a tsunami, and I tried to jerk away from the horrible stench of Cyrus Whitlock's rancid breath, only to find I was tied to a chair.

"*Help*!" I screamed at the top of my lungs. "*Somebody, help me!*"

The evil bastard laughed as he moved across the room,

taking the light with him. "Yell and scream all you want. There's no one around to hear you for miles."

That only made me scream louder, over and over again until my throat felt like I'd swallowed jagged shards of glass.

"More you fight and scream, more fun I'm gonna have breakin' you before I finally end you."

I pulled in a breath on a broken sob as I scanned my surroundings. From what I could see, it looked like we were in a barn, one that had seen better days by the looks and smell of it, and looked like it hadn't been used in quite some time. The chair I was tied to was in the very center of the dusty, straw-covered ground while my captor sat on a stool a few feet in front of me. An old-school fuel lantern, the only means of light in the place, sat on an old, moldy bale of hay beside him. I didn't know how long I'd been unconscious, but the sun coming through the wooden boards was dim and low, like it was making its decent for the evening, leading me to believe that he'd had me for a few hours already.

"Why are you doing this?" I answered, tears clogging my throat.

"Why?" Cyrus asked incredulously before letting out a bark of laughter. "*Why*?" I reared back when he lunged off the stool and got in my face. "Because whores like you need to learn your place!" he shouted, spittle flying from his mouth and landing on my cheek.

"Women were created for breeding and to take care of their menfolk. When you disrespected me, it became clear

I needed to show you the way the world is supposed to work. You've been corrupted. You're a sinner and a whore, and you must be punished."

This guy was officially off his rocker. He had no grasp on reality, and I knew right then and there if I was going to make it out of this alive, I needed to get my shit together and come up with a plan.

I couldn't afford to wait around for someone else to save me. I was going to have to do it myself.

———

Hunter

Knowing that Serenity had been taken was a pain more excruciating than anything I'd ever felt. It was worse than every loss I'd endured. It was like a piece of my very soul was missing, and in the hands of that fucking madman.

When Rory called three hours ago and told me Cyrus Whitlock had kidnapped Serenity, my world stopped spinning, and it hadn't yet started back up.

We'd searched everywhere we could think of. I'd gone back to his trailer, but it was obvious he hadn't returned since I kicked the goddamn door in.

We beat down the door of every known associate he had, to see if someone from that twisted world of his was hiding him.

The police had roadblocks up all around town with a

description of the truck he was driving, but so far it had turned up nothing.

And with each passing second, I unraveled more and more. I had only just gotten her. After wasting so much time playing stupid fucking games, I finally got my head out of my ass and told her what she really meant to me.

And now she was gone.

This couldn't be how our story ended. I had already lost too much in my life, I wasn't going to lose her too.

Moving to where Fletcher sat, curled into himself on one of the barstools in the middle of the Tap Room, I braced my hands on his shoulders until he lifted his head and met my gaze.

The place was a swarm of activity. From police to my brothers at Alpha Omega and all their women, the entire town had shown up, wanting to help with the search.

Stella was doing her best to remain calm, but I could see the panic etched into her face in the form of lines that hadn't been there before. She was holding on as hard as she could but was losing her grip. I needed to end this for her and the rest of her family before she lost her battle and caved in on herself.

"I know I asked you this already son, but I need you to think hard. Is there anywhere you can think of that your old man might've taken her? Anywhere off the beaten path, some place we haven't looked."

The poor kid was white as a sheet and shaking uncontrollably. His lips parted slightly as he started to shake his head only to stop and widen his eyes like something had just dawned on him.

"There's one place," he started, trailing off as his eyes grew distant with thought.

I gave him a little shake to bring him back to the present as desperation clawed my insides to shreds. "Where? Fletcher, think hard."

His gaze cleared and returned to mine. "I heard my dad and one of his friends talk about it a few times, years ago. It's a bad place."

My stomach sank. "Tell me where it is."

————

Serenity

The longer I spent in that goddamn barn, the clearer it became that something in his brain had snapped, and he was never coming back from it. He paced the length of the barn. Back and forth, back and forth. Over and over as he rambled on and on about the scourge of society, and how the world was burning and hellfire.

As he ranted and raged, I worked at the ropes twisted around my wrists, tying my hands behind my back. I could feel the skin tearing from the abrasive material, and the blood dripping down my fingers onto the filthy ground below, but I didn't stop. If I was going to get out of this, I only had one shot. I needed to make it count.

My heart was in my throat, my bottom lip clamped between my teeth to keep from crying out in pain as I fought against the ropes.

But I eventually felt them loosen, and my hands broke free.

I could have cried in relief, but I had to figure out what to do about my feet that were tied to the chair legs.

I shifted my weight from side to side, testing the chair's durability and discovered it didn't have much. The best bet I had would be to break it. Odds were, it was going to hurt like hell, but I couldn't let that stop me.

Any moment now he was going to remember he had me tied up and at his mercy; I needed to act before that happened.

Squeezing my eyes closed and sucking in a fortifying breath, I silently counted down from three in my head. When I reached one, I pushed up with my feet as high as I could and threw myself backward, bending my neck forward to keep from whacking the back of my head on the unforgiving ground.

I crashed down on my back, the impact so jarring it knocked the air from my lungs, but it worked. I heard the cracking and splintering of the wood and immediately began to wriggle and kick my legs free.

I heard Cyrus's bellow and the thunder of his boots on the packed ground and reached down for one of the broken chair legs. As soon as his form appeared over me, I swung as hard as I could, like my life depended on it.

My aim was off from the rattle my body just took, and

I got him in his side, but it was enough to knock him back so I could scurry to my feet.

I had just enough time to raise the chair leg like it was a baseball bat before he righted himself and looked at me with pure, unadulterated evil in his eyes.

With a roar that sent fear spiking through my blood, he lunged at me, but I was ready, and this time, my aim was true.

I got him across the side of his head, the crack of the wood against his skull so loud it made my stomach roil.

His body twisted around at the force of the impact, and he went down like a ton of bricks. I didn't know if I'd knocked him unconscious or worse, and I didn't have time to find out, because when he fell, he knocked into the hay bale sending the lantern flying. It shattered against the ground in a burst of fire that spread faster than I thought was possible but given that everything in the bar was long dead and dried out, it made the perfect kindling, and in a matter of seconds, the fire spread.

The smoke was thick and black, heavy and acrid, and my eyes immediately began to water as I covered my mouth and coughed.

I started for the door when I heard the sound of pained moans over the crackling of the flames and the screaming of the wood as it burned.

I looked back to see Cyrus trying to rise to his hands and knees, and in that moment, there was a part of me that felt like I needed to go back and help him; I couldn't leave him in this burning tinder box.

I barely made it a step in his direction when a wall of flame shot up between us.

I had no choice. I couldn't stay in here a second long. I was on the right side of that fire, the path to freedom clear for me. He was already trapped, so as hard a choice as it was to make, I spun back around and fled.

———

Hunter

The dark sky danced with orange and yellow as we flew up the road to the barn Fletcher had remembered. It belonged to one of Cyrus's old buddies and from what Fletcher said went on in there, I knew it was a place of nightmares, ones that were worse that the dreams I'd been plagued with for so many years.

Sirens screamed all around me as the long line of cars trailing my truck followed my lead and whipped off the road into the overgrown field.

The barn was fully engulfed, flames spitting out everywhere, and the sight of my old enemy made my throat close up. No one could have survived that, and my heart nearly stopped beating at the thought that Serenity could be inside.

My Wildcat.

The woman I wanted to spend the rest of my life with.

But just before I could lose it completely, I caught

sight of a silhouette standing in the field, long hair whipping in the breeze as she stared at the burning barn.

I pulled up beside her in a flash before slamming on the brakes. Throwing the truck into park, I shot out, her name a shout bursting past my lips.

Her head came around, those beautiful eyes slamming into me like a Mack truck. "Hunter," she breathed as soon as I reached her.

"I thought I lost you," I rasped as I clasped her face in my hands and crouched down to inspect as much of her as I could in the light of the blazing inferno. "God, I thought I lost you."

"I-I'm okay," she said with a croak before burying her face in my chest and bursting into tears. Her arms came around me, squeezing so tight it was hard to breathe, but I didn't care. She was alive and in my arms, where she was safe.

I let her absorb all the warmth and comfort I had to give, wrapping her safely in my embrace as her body trembled while Leo and Micah, Linc, Bryce, the rest of my family and the police from the Hope Valley department surrounded us like they were creating a protective bubble.

We stayed like that until I felt her trembling stop and her tears dried up. "Baby, what happened? Where's Cyrus?"

She tilted her chin at the barn. "He's in there. I-I tried to go back for him." She shook her head like it was the most ridiculous thing she'd ever heard. "I hated him so much, but I couldn't leave him to burn up like that." A single tear tracked down her cheek. "But it was too late. I couldn't get him out, not without getting trapped myself."

"Hey." I clasped her chin between my fingers and tipped her face to mine. Even with streaks of black smoke dusting her face, I didn't think she'd ever been more beautiful. "I don't want you to give that fucker another thought, you hear me? You made the right decision, saving yourself, and I don't want you to *ever* doubt that. That man was pure evil, and the world is better off without him in it."

She sniffled and nodded her head before lowering her forehead against my chest and fisting the front of my shirt in her hands.

"What can I do, baby? Tell me what I need to do to make you feel better."

"Take me home," she replied without missing a beat.

She didn't have to ask twice.

————

The first rays of early morning sunlight started pouring through my front window just as the last of our family and friends left, confident I'd be able to give Serenity whatever she needed to get her past this nightmare.

Once the fire department showed up on the scene and put the fire out, the barn was little more than rubble. I hadn't stuck around to see it, of course, because the moment Serenity asked me to take her home, I had her loaded in my truck and we were driving the hell out of that field.

Leo and Micah showed up a couple hours later to get Serenity's statement so they could put the case to bed. Sure enough, the bastard's body had been found among the charred rubble, but I couldn't find it in myself to care.

Turned out, my Wildcat had lived up to her title, saving herself before we'd even known where to look.

She'd managed to free herself and fought back, fought for her life.

The fire was nothing more than an accident that couldn't have been avoided. I knew she'd be haunted by what went down in that barn for a while, but there wasn't anything I wouldn't do to guide her out of the shadows and into the light. After all, she'd done the very same for me.

After she recounted everything in vivid detail, she'd climbed in the shower to wash the smoke and dirt off, and then proceeded to pass out in my bed.

I'd left her to it, knowing sleep was exactly what she needed at the time.

Her family hung around for hours, as well as every brother from Alpha Omega and their wives. They needed to be in her space, to know she was okay, and I didn't mind one damn bit giving them that.

Halfway through the night, a knock sounded on the door, and Stella opened it to reveal Fletcher standing on my front porch, looking ravaged.

"Is she okay?" he'd asked, his voice breaking.

He didn't ask about his father, not once.

I took him back to see her, knowing that was what it was going to take for him to be certain she was safe. Together, we'd watched her sleep for a couple minutes before heading back into the living room.

He'd tried leaving, but the women, sensing he was blaming himself for everything that had gone down, refused to let him hold on to the guilt that wasn't his to carry. Instead of letting him leave, they'd dragged him into the kitchen and coddled him like a bunch of momma hens, giving him exactly what he needed until the shadows in his eyes faded away.

Now, as Serenity slept in our bed, Fletcher was crashed out on the couch, sleeping soundly with the knowledge that his favorite person in the world was going to be all right.

I stood at the front window, eyeing the trees surrounding my property, searching for a bit of peace. I didn't know how long I'd remained there when I felt Serenity's delicate hand come to rest on my forearm before sliding down and twining her fingers between mine.

"I'd ask what's got you thinking so hard, but I'm pretty sure I already know the answer to that."

I turned to her, pulling her against me and locking her in my embrace as I inhaled deeply, filling my lungs with the scent of jasmine.

"All I could think was that I lost you."

"But you didn't," she whispered, tilting her head back

to look at me as she rested her palms on my chest. "I'm right here, and I'm not going anywhere."

"Promise me that," I demanded.

"What?"

"Promise you're not going anyway. Marry me, Sere. Be my wife."

"I—"

"It's what I need. It's the only thing that's going to make me feel better after driving up and seeing that goddamn barn burning. I need you to promise you'll be mine forever, so marry me."

As far as proposals went, I was sure it wasn't the most romantic one out there, but it was the truth.

Her hazel eyes swam with unshed tears. "You want to marry me?"

I trailed my fingers down her hair in a gentle caress. "Wildcat, it's the only thing I'll ever want, because as long as I have you, I've got everything I need. You're it, baby."

For the first time in hours, she smiled that heart-stopping smile, and just like that, I knew we were going to be all right.

"Well, when you put it like that, how could I possibly turn you down?"

I felt a chuckle rumble up my chest as she chased away the last of the shadows and filled my world with sunlight. "You could try, but I'm nothing if not determined."

She laughed, full and happy.

"Yes, Hunter. I'll marry you. It's all I ever want."

And with that, she made everything better.

EPILOGUE
SERENITY

F *our years later*

"Fletcher Whitlock."

At the sound of his name being called by the dean and the sight of him walking across that stage to get his diploma, the not-so-small entourage from Hope Valley that had made the trek to watch our boy graduate exploded in cheers and whoops that reverberated through the stadium.

I could have sworn I saw Fletcher's cheeks tinge pink even though he was so far away.

Tears of happiness swelled in my eyes before falling down my cheeks as our cheers finally tapered off and we all sat back down to watch the rest of the college graduates take their walk across the stage.

My heart was so full at that moment, I wasn't sure what to do with everything I was feeling. As I stared at Fletcher, it was hard to believe that, only four years ago, he'd been this scrawny, beaten-down boy living in constant fear. He didn't look like the same person. My boy grew up to be a looker, I'll tell you that. And with those looks were brains and heart.

He liked to say that I helped, but he'd done it all himself. And I couldn't have been prouder.

"Daddy, Mommy's cwyin' again."

At my little girl's proclamation, Hunter turned to find me bawling like a baby as I clutched the program to my chest with both hands.

"Aw, is my Wildcat deep in her feelings again today?"

I sniffled and batted at my cheeks as I shot him a glare. "I can't help it," I said on a pout as I rested a hand on my extremely round belly. "It's all your fault. You know what my hormones are like when I'm pregnant."

After all, we'd already done this once. Our little Gracie had come squalling into the world nearly three years ago, and the whole time I'd been pregnant with her, I'd been an absolute basket case.

He patted my belly and smiled down at me with a look of adoration that made me weak in the knees. "And until you push our little man out, I will gladly take the blame for anything you want to throw at me."

It had to be said, not only was Hunter the world's very best husband, he was also a pretty kickass father as well. But I'd already known that from how he was with his own boys.

Speaking of, Liam leaned forward so he could see me past his big brother and Uncle Hunt. "Don't worry, Aunt Sere. We'll stop on the way home and get you all the ice cream. How's that sound?"

"Like heaven. You know you're my favorite, right?"

Luke rolled his eyes, knowing I switch favorites more than most people changed their underwear.

I'd worried for a while what would happen to Hunter's relationship with the boys after he made it clear to Vera he wasn't going to be the backup plan any longer, but it was a testament to how he'd helped raise them that they'd grown up to be good, solid men with big hearts.

He might not have had a relationship with their mother any longer, but Luke and Liam had made it clear that Hunter was their family, and there wasn't anything anyone could do to change that. He was their constant.

That meant, as the years passed, my relationship with them grew even stronger, and now they were a part of our family in an even bigger way.

Gracie already had them both wrapped around her little finger, and I couldn't wait to see how they'd behave when our little man came into the world in a few short months.

It wasn't surprising that Vera's second marriage hadn't

lasted long, after all, if a woman could make eyes at another man on her wedding day, it didn't say good things about the man she was pledging herself to. She and Oliver divorced in less than a year, but she'd quickly moved on to someone else. I didn't know what she was searching for, but I hoped she eventually found it.

Stella's head peeked out from the other side of her husband. "Did someone say ice cream?" she asked as she rubbed her own pregnant belly.

While Hunter and I were on baby number two, jumping into our lives together headfirst, West and Stella had taken things a little slower, wading in comfortably. She was currently pregnant with their first baby. A boy who was due only a week after mine.

And just like their moms, I knew they were going to be the very best of friends.

When I first moved to Hope Valley, and I'd been looking for a fresh start, a new life. But never in a million years did I think I'd end up this blessed.

My husband turned to me then, his icy blue eyes swimming with sunshine, not a single shadow in sight.

"You happy, baby?"

I smiled up at him, warmth spreading through my entire body. "Every single day."

The End.

Thank you so much for sticking with me through this series. These characters and this town are truly special. Be sure to check out the NOTE FROM THE AUTHOR at the front of the book for more HV news.

In the mean time, keep reading if you're not in the mood to leave Hope Valley just yet.

Enjoy an Excerpt of Bombshell

If you're not quite ready to leave Hope Valley behind yet, then check out my Whiskey Dolls series, featuring the dancers from Virginia's top burlesque club!
You'll get peeks at some of your favorite Hope Valley characters as well.

Chapter 1

Marin

"Welcome to Cooking Solo," the tall, reed-thin woman at the front of the room announced in a voice that rang with so much cheer, it screamed of bullshit. "A class designed for singles, such as yourselves, who want to learn the art of cooking for one."

And this is what my life has become, I thought glumly, *being passive-aggressively judged by a stick figure with a carat-and-a-half rock on her ring finger.*

There should have been some sort of disclaimer when I signed up for the class online stating the instructor was a "happily married mother of three."

If you were going to be teaching people to cook for one because they were painfully and glaringly *A-L-O-N-E,* the least you could do was be single yourself.

But oh no, Chef Jodi—a title she'd undoubtedly christened herself with and insisted we call her by—couldn't stop talking about her loving husband and precious babies.

I kind of hated Chef Jodi. Chef Jodi was an asshole.

"Now, we're going to start off simple, because the last thing any single man or woman probably wants to do is waste time in the kitchen cooking up some complicated dish just for themselves, am I right?" She let out a condescending laugh. "I'm sure you'd rather be on one of those Tinder apps or on a blind date or whatever it is you single people do nowadays to try to meet someone."

I was going to smack the shit out of this woman with

my handy little spatula the next time she came around to my station.

"So tonight, I'm going to teach you to make one of my husband's favorite meals—"

The vibe in the room was growing more hostile the longer she rattled on, and something told me Chef Jodi was going to be getting some pretty nasty reviews on Yelp.

"For the love of God, Jodi," a woman who looked to be in her sixties, one station across and back from mine, declared. "We *all* know you and your family. Your husband spends so much time in his damn recliner doin' a whole lotta nothing that his ass is permanently flattened. Those *sweet little angels* you're goin' on about nearly started a forest fire last summer with a bunch of illegal fireworks, and everyone in town knows you lock yourself in the bathroom with a bottle of wine and sleep in the bathtub at least once a week just to escape the chaos. So you can get the hell off your high horse, already."

The laugh I tried to swallow down came out as a snort as the room filled with snickers from all directions.

With Jodi properly put in her place, she managed to go about teaching the rest of the lesson without any more insults, and we were able to go about making our rosemary chicken without the commentary on how much her husband loved it.

I wasn't a very good cook, so for the past few months I'd been living off cereal, boxes of powdered mac and cheese, and soup from a can—another reason I'd stupidly thought signing up for Cooking Solo was a good idea.

By the end of the class, I'd succeeded in making a passable dish that didn't smell like charred feet and was only slightly rubbery, so I was feeling pretty good about myself as I cleaned my station and packed up to head home. Then I turned around and lost my breath at the sight of the man at one of the stations near the back of the room.

Pierce Walton: the sexiest man in existence, successful lawyer, single father of what had to be the cutest little boy on the face of the planet, world-class prick, and the older brother of my abusive asshole of an ex-boyfriend.

Well shit.

My feet were rooted to the floor for the several seconds it took my brain to reengage after short circuiting— because that was the kind of effect the man had on pretty much everyone, men and women alike.

Before he could look up and spot me, I ducked behind a group of fellow singles and booked it for the side exit as my heart beat wildly, attempting to escape the confines of my chest.

As soon as I rounded the corner, I plastered my back to the wall, breathing like I'd just run a mile at a dead sprint. I chanced a quick peek, unable to help myself where Pierce was concerned. From the very first moment I'd met him, the man had some kind of crazy power over me. Inappropriate as hell, given that I'd been in a relationship with his little brother at the time. But it couldn't be helped. There was just something about him, he was a freaking wizard or something.

A few people passed by, giving me strange looks, but I

couldn't bring myself to care. I tried to be as inconspicuous as possible as I leaned farther for a better look. Just another inch . . . and there he was. God, the man still took my breath away.

It really was too bad we hated each other.

In my defense, my hatred of him was solely reactionary. He'd hated me first, so I figured it was only fair I hate the stupid sexy jerk back. I'd have been fine with the guy if he hadn't decided within the first half hour of meeting me that I was somehow seriously lacking for whatever reason.

I'd been dating Frank for six months when he'd taken me to meet his family for the very first time. I was standing in his mother's kitchen, helping with the last-minute preparations of the very lovely dinner she'd made, when the back door suddenly opened and a Grecian god came waltzing through.

I was stunned into immobility at the mere sight of him. In his expensive-looking suit and well-polished shoes, he looked like he belonged on the glossy pages of a magazine, modeling men's designer clothes, not stepping into a small, countrified home in a small mountain town. Then I looked down to the little toddler holding his hand, a near spitting image of the dark and dangerous man who'd just come in, and nearly swooned into a puddle of goo.

The only way I could describe how I felt in that moment was *dazzled*. I was completely dazzled by this gorgeous stranger while standing in the kitchen of my boyfriend's childhood home.

He looked up at me with eyes so blue they glinted like

glaciers in the middle of the sea, and for a beat, he seemed almost as flummoxed as I was. There was something in his penetrating gaze that I wasn't able to read, but whatever it was, it had warmed me to my core. It made me fidgety and antsy. I wanted to dive in and get to know him at the very same time a tiny voice in the back of my head was telling me to run away because this man was Dangerous with a capital D.

We stood there, staring at each other in surprise for what felt like an eternity before Mrs. Walton cleared her throat and broke the spell. Then he smiled a smile that rattled me to my very core.

"Well, hello there," he said in a velvety smooth voice that had just the right amount of delicious rasp to it. "I'm Pierce." He extended the hand not attached to the adorable kid, and the instant his long, thick fingers engulfed my hand, goosebumps broke out across my whole body. "And who might you be?"

His mother jumped to introduce me when it became obvious the power of speech had failed me, and as soon as the words, "Frank's girlfriend" left her mouth, a switch flipped. The man who'd nearly knocked me on my ass just a minute earlier with nothing more than a smile was suddenly giving me the deep freeze.

Every encounter after that was downright chilly. Every forced conversation felt layered with frost until I eventually just gave up all together.

Frank used to bad mouth his brother constantly, always going on about how arrogant and condescending he was, how he thought he was better because he'd gone to law school and worked in the city. The colder Pierce acted toward me, the easier it was to understand Frank's animosity toward his big brother, and eventually, Frank's animosity became my own.

Once again my breath caught in my throat as I watched him. With the sleeves of his expensive button-down rolled to mid-forearm, I was able to stare, transfixed, at the cords and muscles flexing and straining beneath his golden-tanned skin as he wiped down his prep station.

The last place I'd ever expected to see Pierce was at a cooking class. It was a complete contradiction to the callous man I knew him to be.

His hair flopped down over his forehead as he leaned over, adding a boyish element to the man's hard, chiseled face that managed to somehow soften his granite-like features just a bit. I hadn't thought it possible for the man to ever look soft. He always seemed to be in a bad mood. In the three years I'd dated his douchebag of a brother, I'd only been around Pierce a handful of times and, with the exception of that very first encounter in his mom's kitchen, I'd never seen the man smile.

On top of hard, brooding features, he had the most incredible icy blue eyes I'd ever seen. They had the ability to freeze a person to their core with just one look. I knew that for a fact, considering after each run-in with the glacial man I felt like I had frostbite.

Still, as much as it irked me, I couldn't help being fascinated by him.

"Uh . . . everything okay here?" I jerked up, whipping back around so fast my hair slapped me in my face when I turned to the woman standing a few feet away. She lowered her voice to a conspiratorial whisper as she looked off in the direction I'd just been staring. "Do you need me to call the police or something?"

"What? No! Oh God. No. Sorry. I just—" I stopped myself mid-ramble and held my hands out, palms up. "No, sorry. Everything's fine. I just spotted someone I know, and I didn't want him to see me, so I'm hiding."

Oh great, Marin. Because that admission totally doesn't make you sound like a wackadoodle.

Her brows climbed higher on her forehead. "Why didn't you just leave then?"

I gave a small, self-deprecating laugh. "Well, because I didn't want *him* to see *me*. But *I* still wanted to see *him*, you know?" Realizing how that sounded, I quickly added, "But not in a weird way! In a totally normal, non-creepy kind of way."

I'll take Things Stalkers Say for a thousand, Alex.

If anything, the woman looked even more convinced that she needed to call the police.

I pulled in a slow, steady breath in an attempt to calm my nerves that had been firing like crazy since I saw Pierce, and explained, "He's my ex-boyfriend's older brother."

Understanding lit her eyes, and the panicked look of *I'm standing here talking to a psycho* drifted away. "Ah. I see." She joined me at the wall and peeked around with me to get a better look. "Wow," she breathed. "He's very good looking."

"Yeah," I said with a defeated sigh. "The stupid jerk." She looked back to me, a quizzical brow arched in suspicion. "Sorry. It's a long story. I should probably get out of here before he notices me. Is he looking this way?"

The woman glanced back. "No—wait." She watched for another second before whispering, "Okay, go!"

"Thanks," I whispered back, pushing off the wall and scuttling down the hallway.

"Have a good evening. See you next class," she continued to whisper-yell.

"Yeah, you too," I returned, waving over my shoulder.

Half an hour ago I'd been so sure I was done with Cooking Solo and that snooty Chef Jodi. But then I saw him. And even though I couldn't stand the guy, I knew that if it meant I'd get another chance to gawk when he wasn't looking, I'd be returning for the next class.

Because I was nothing if not a glutton for punishment.

CLICK HERE TO KEEP READING

MORE FROM HOPE VALLEY

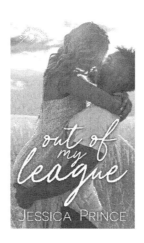

After years of war, Lincoln Sheppard thought he'd left the violence and ugliness behind. He was content with the life he built for himself. Then the woman down the street came in and shook everything up.

All Eden Brenner ever wanted was to have a place to call home. She finally found that in Hope Valley. Then she went and fell in love with the man a few houses down the first time she laid eyes on him. There was just one problem. Women like her didn't catch the attention of men like him. He was totally and completely out of her league. And to make matters worse, when her past comes knocking, the beautiful world she's built for herself is at risk of crumbling to the ground.

When danger forces Eden into his arms, Lincoln begins to see her in a whole new light, and he suddenly finds himself wanting things he never expected. And he wants them all with the shy, clumsy woman from down the street. But when the truth comes out, that proves nearly impossible. Now he's fighting the hardest battle of his life, and the stakes are higher than ever. Protect the woman he's falling for while trying to win her heart at the same time.

———

Temperance Levine had her entire world ripped away from her at eighteen. What had once been a life full of light and happiness was torn to shreds in the blink of an eye. With nothing left but a broken heart and painful memories, she ran away from the only home she'd ever had and tried to start over somewhere else. But the grass isn't always greener on the other side, and sometimes all you can do to heal old wounds is come back home again.

The day Temperance left him was the worst day of Hayes Walker's life, and he'd spent every one since then merely existing. The future he'd imagined had gone up in smoke, and all he could do was take life one step at a time. But when tragedy brings Tempie back to Hope Valley, he knows this is the only shot he'll have at getting his happiness back, and there's no way he'll let this chance go to waste.

After years apart, Tempie and Hayes are finally starting over and looking toward the future. But when their sleepy little town is rocked to its core, Hayes will be forced into a battle he never saw coming. Now he's not only fighting for the future he always dreamed of, but also trying to protect the only woman he's ever loved.

It wasn't hard for Nona Fanning to fall for Trick. He was strong, kind-hearted, loyal, and unbelievably handsome. He was the man of her dreams, and all it took was one night to give her a taste of the beauty he had to offer. But while she'd been opening her heart to him, he'd kept his under lock and key.

After Patrick "Trick" Wanderly's wife left him, ripping away their picture-perfect life, he convinced himself that she'd taken the best pieces of him with her. He wasn't ready to move on and give his heart to someone else. Then his whole world flipped upside down after spending one night with Nona.

It took awhile for him to see what he had standing right in front of him, but now Trick's eyes are open, and he's determined to fix what he broke. But when danger threatens to tear Nona's world apart, it's up to Trick to help hold those pieces together while fighting to protect the woman and the new life he's come to cherish.

Gypsy Bradbury was never destined for great things. Or at least that's what she'd convinced herself of. Growing up on the wrong side of the tracks, she had learned that hoping for more was a waste of time. Then Marco forced his way into her life and gave her a glimpse of a future brighter than any she could have imagined. But if her past taught her anything, it was that if something seemed too good to be true... it probably was.

The promise of a quiet, simple life was what drew Marco Castillo to Hope Valley. After experiencing war and death first hand, he was looking for something easy. Then he met a woman with guarded eyes and the most beautiful smile he'd ever seen. The only problem was she came with more baggage than a 747.

There is nothing easy about Gypsy, but Marco knows without a doubt that the promise of her is well worth the effort. She's the strongest, bravest woman he's ever met, and when the life she's fought to build for her and her family is threatened, Marco is determined to win that battle for her. Whether Gypsy wants his help or not.

———

Rory Hightower had a good life. She had a loving family, great friends, and a job she adored, running Hope Valley's local watering hole, The Tap Room. But there was just one thing missing. Ever since she was a little girl she knew there was one special guy out there just for her. Her dream man. And when Cord walked into her bar, she knew instantly it was him. Which made losing him all the more painful.

Cord Paulson had only ever had one person he could depend on. And that bond ran deep. But when he moved to Hope Valley and met the breathtaking bartender with the bright blue eyes and stunning smile, he felt an instant connection. He wanted Rory from the moment he laid eyes on her. But when his past came back and his loyalties were put to the test, he made the biggest mistake of his life.

Then one night changes everything. After avoiding him for months, Rory has no choice but to lower her guard and let him back in. And Cord plans to use that to his full advantage. He's determined to repair the damage he caused to her heart and win her back. He may have lost the love of his life once already, but there's no way he'll make the same mistake twice.

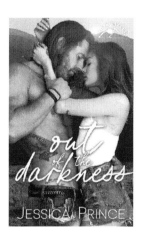

The light had been snuffed out of Xander Caine's world a long time ago, leaving him to suffer in darkness. After a tremendous loss, he closed himself off from anyone and everyone, content to live alone in the shadows. Then a woman blew into town with the force of a hurricane and shook everything up.

Sage Winthrop was looking to start over. She didn't have a plan for what her new life would look like, but when she landed in Hope Valley, she knew it was the place she wanted to call home. Then one chance encounter outside of the best coffee shop in town set her world spinning.

Sage and Xander hated each other on sight. However, when they're forced to work together, that hate eventually turns into something neither of them expected. Their attraction proves too strong to ignore. But when secrets from Sage's past are revealed and her life is threatened, Xander has no choice but to let go of his demons and step out of the darkness in order to save the woman he loves.

———

Tessa Day had clung to the notion of a once-in-a-lifetime love for as long as she could remember. Then one chance encounter led her to the man of her dreams. After a whirlwind romance that could only be described as something out of a fairytale, she gave her heart to her other half, only to have him throw it back like it meant nothing.

Bryce Dixon was known as the care-free funny guy with a heart of gold. But it was all a façade. For more than ten years, he'd been holding on to guilt that was slowly eating him alive. He blamed himself for things in his past, and as punishment for his sins, he walked away from the only woman he'd ever loved.

But when Tessa shows up in Hope Valley, Bryce begins to think that maybe he's been given a second chance. However, when danger comes calling, he soon discovers he's in for the fight of his life. Not only does he have to protect the woman who holds his heart, but he also has to convince her that he can get things right the second time around.

After a bitter divorce had left him jaded and cynical, Leo Drake thought he was done. To him, love and happiness were myths. Then the shy, sweet, coffee shop owner looked up at him with those big gray eyes and beautiful smile, and he was done for.

Danika Parrish had been the nerdy girl growing up. The girl who sat in her window, watching the boy across the street, and secretly longing for the day when he might notice her. When that day finally came, she was convinced all her dreams had come true. But after giving her everything she'd ever hoped for, he'd ripped it all away with a handful of words.

Leo's made a lot of mistakes in his life, but the one he regrets most is hurting Danika. For the first time in his life, he knows what it feels like to love someone, to truly be happy, and he'll do whatever it takes to win her back. He's determined to prove to her that he's worth a second chance. That he's the forever she's been waiting all her life for.

———

After her husband left her for her best friend, Hayden Young moved to Hope Valley looking for a fresh start for her and her daughter. The last thing she expected was to run into the man who had rocked her world in the middle of the wine section of the local grocery store. And no matter how many times she tells herself she hates the egotistical jerk, she can't stop the tingle she feels every time she looks at him.

Micah Langford was a man who enjoyed variety. He had absolutely no interest in finding one woman and settling down. Then a one-night-stand from his past—and the best sex of his life—came rolling into town, and the self-proclaimed bachelor started wanting more. The only problem is, she can't stand the sight of him.

When hate gives way to fire, igniting a passion neither of them can deny, Micah finds himself thinking about the future—or more specifically, how he can fit Hayden into his. But when a case he's working on heats up, and she starts asking questions he can't answer, Hayden has a decision to make. She can either take a leap and put her trust in him, or she can let the secrets destroy them.

When it came to the men in her life, Charlotte Belmont was cursed. She'd known losers, cheaters, abusers, and criminals, so it went without saying, she stopped trusting her judgment a long time ago. Then Dalton came into her life; a good, dependable man who made her heart race and her body hot. When she felt herself falling for him, she did the only thing she could think to protect them both . . . she ran like hell.

Dalton Prescott was a protector by nature, so when the woman he'd been tasked to keep safe was almost killed on his watch, he carried that guilt like a weight on his shoulders. What made matters worse was that before everything went south, Dalton had started to care for Charlotte in a way that had nothing to do with his job.

She's determined to ignore their attraction and keep him at a distance, but he's playing for keeps and has no intention of losing. However, when ghosts from the past start popping up, bringing with them a whole new threat, Dalton may be the only man who can keep her safe this time.

———

The last thing Stella Ryan had time for was a man. With her family in trouble and looking to her to fix everything, romance and commitment were the furthest things from her mind. Until she ran into a man with a jawline that could cut granite and arms she wanted to lick like an ice cream cone. A man who made her forget the things that really mattered.

West Scott was one of the last bachelors standing. With all his Alpha Omega brothers settling down and popping out a bunch of kids, he had become the target for meddling women looking to fix him up. But there was one woman, in particular, he couldn't get out of his head. The one in the killer dress with a gift for picking pockets.

When fate puts Stella in his path again, he's determined to get to the cause of her desperation and help solve all her problems. If only the headstrong, stubborn woman would let him in. She's trying her hardest to keep her walls up, but he's dead set on showing her that the best things happen when you least expect it.

ABOUT JESSICA

Born and raised around Houston, Jessica is a self proclaimed caffeine addict, connoisseur of inexpensive wine, and the worst driver in the state of Texas. In addition to being all of these things, she's first and foremost a wife and mom.

Growing up, she shared her mom and grandmother's love of reading. But where they leaned toward murder mysteries, Jessica was obsessed with all things romance.

When she's not nose deep in her next manuscript, you can usually find her with her kindle in hand.

Connect with Jessica now
Website: www.authorjessicaprince.com
Jessica's Princesses Reader Group
Newsletter
Instagram
Facebook
Twitter
authorjessicaprince@gmail.com

Printed in Great Britain
by Amazon

28289537R00175